The Other Brother

Book 4

in the *Chop, Chop* Series

by
L.N. Cronk

Front Cover Photography by Konstantin Inozemtsev.
Back Cover Photography by Stefan Klein.

ISBN Number: 978-0-9820027-3-5

Published by Rivulet Publishing
West Jefferson, NC, 28694, U.S.A.

For Becky, Dargan, Deacon, Jenna, Kyle, Lee, and Oisìn.

For physical training is of some value, but godliness has value for all things, holding promise for both the present life and the life to come. - 1 Timothy 4:8

~ ~ ~

I'VE KNOWN CHARLOTTE ever since she was a toddler – when she and her brother, Greg, first moved into town. I was twelve years old at the time and Greg quickly became my best friend – so she's been like a little sister to me for a long time.

As a matter of fact, she and her mom are like family to me. This has *always* been true – ever since I've known them.

But it's been especially true since Greg and their dad died.

And Charlotte's been through a lot (I guess we both have), so I've always tried to be there for her . . . like a big brother would be.

Don't get me wrong – I'd never try to take Greg's place.

But I guess you could say that I'm her *other* brother.

I guess you could also say that's why I was lugging what seemed like everything Charlotte had ever owned up five flights of stairs. It was freshman move-in day at State, and of course I'd agreed to help. Her mom and Tanner were helping too, and we'd all soon realized that it was going to be a whole lot quicker to take the stairs than to wait in line for one of the two ancient elevators that serviced Charlotte's dorm.

I set a box down and looked around her crowded little room, wondering where in the world she was going to put everything. Tanner barged in, showing off by carrying a large box on each shoulder.

Tanner was a lot like a brother to Charlotte too. Of course he wasn't as close to her as *I* was, but he was practically her brother-in-law. His youngest brother, Jordan, was dating Charlotte and, although they hadn't been going out all that long, it was pretty much a given that one day they'd get married.

"What's that?" I asked Tanner, pointing to one of the boxes. "Her lead-weight collection?"

1

"Probably," he said, not laughing as he set one box down and then the other.

"Everything okay?" I asked. He'd been unusually quiet all day.

"Yup," he said, heading back out for another load before I could question him any further.

I headed out the door after him, figuring he was just missing Jordan more than he'd anticipated. A week earlier Jordan had boarded a plane for Texas where he'd received a full baseball scholarship. If he hadn't gotten that scholarship, he'd be going to State too, right here with Charlotte.

Charlotte hugged Tanner goodbye first, then turned to me.

"You be *careful!*" I told her.

"Yes, Father," she said, bowing her head contritely.

"I'm serious," I said. "You need to stay focused on why you're here and put the ax to the grind stone."

"*Put the ax to the grind stone?*" she asked. "Who says that?"

"People say that," I told her.

"Not anymore," she said. "Honestly, what century were you born in?"

"Same one as you, dearie."

"You'd never know it," she muttered, but then she looked at me seriously. "Don't worry. I'm not gonna screw up."

During her junior year in high school – just before she'd started dating Jordan – Charlotte had gotten pregnant. She'd had the baby, put it up for adoption, graduated second in her class, and managed to salvage her relationship with Jordan, but it hadn't been an easy time – for any of us. I knew she still felt bad about what everyone had gone through because of it.

"I know you're not gonna screw up," I said. "That's not what I meant. Just . . . just *be careful.* I worry about you."

"Okay," she nodded, giving me a tight hug.

She turned to her mom who was already wiping away a tear.

2

"I'm coming home in a week, Mom!"

"I know," Mrs. White said. "I'm sorry. I promised myself I wasn't going to cry."

"It's a good thing I'm not the one who went to school in Texas," she said. "You people would be a real mess!"

"I love you." Mrs. White gave her one last hug.

"I love you too," Charlotte said, and we got in Tanner's truck and pulled away.

"I think she was a little teary there herself," I remarked and Mrs. White nodded.

"How long do you think it'll be before she calls?" I asked.

"Five minutes," Mrs. White said.

"I think three."

"Ten," Tanner guessed. "She's gonna call Jordan first."

"This is probably true," I agreed. "It's been a whole forty minutes since she talked to him."

"She talked to him about five times on the ride up here," Mrs. White said. They'd ridden separately in Charlotte's car so she'd have a vehicle at school to get around in.

"How's he liking things down there so far?" I asked Tanner.

"Okay, I guess," he said, shrugging.

"Is everything all right?" Mrs. White asked. Apparently she'd also noticed that he wasn't acting like himself.

"Oh, yeah," he said nonchalantly. "I'm just tired, that's all."

"You didn't have to spend your day doing this," Mrs. White said. "I'm sorry."

"Oh, no, no. I'm fine," Tanner said. "I just . . . I just didn't sleep good last night. I'm fine."

Mrs. White's phone rang.

"Two minutes," I said, looking at my watch. "I win."

Two hours later, we dropped Mrs. White off and then Tanner drove me to my house. He turned into the driveway and then surprised me by shutting the motor off.

"You wanna come in?" I asked. "Laci's probably got dinner ready and I'm sure she'd be glad to–"

"No," he said, shaking his head.

"Well, all right. I guess I'll see you later then." I reached for the door handle.

"Wait."

I let go of the handle and looked at him.

"I need to talk to you about something."

"What?" I asked, figuring he had great plans for a hunting trip or something rolling around in his head.

"Um . . . I've kinda got some bad news."

That's when I realized that he'd said he *needed* to talk with me . . . not that he *wanted* to talk with me. That's also when I realized I was about to find out why he'd been so quiet all day.

"What?"

"Chase came to see me and mom the other day," Tanner said. Chase was Tanner and Jordan's middle brother. He lived about five hours away in Chicago, and he hardly ever came home except for holidays.

"Chase?"

"Yeah."

"What's going on?"

"He's um . . . he's sick."

"He's sick?"

"Yeah."

"What's wrong?"

Tanner hesitated for a moment.

"Ever heard of Huntington's disease?" he finally asked.

Huntington's disease . . . Huntington's disease. I guess maybe I'd *heard* of it, but I certainly couldn't tell you the first thing about it.

"I don't think so," I said, shaking my head. "Not really."

4

"It's a degenerative, neurological disease. It kind of affects everything in the brain . . . movement, like Parkinson's does and mental abilities and emotions . . ."

We both knew a bit about Parkinson's because Natalie's dad had it. Natalie was Tanner's girlfriend and one of Laci's best friends. Her dad had been getting worse lately . . . as a matter of fact, Natalie had just moved back to Cavendish to help her mother take care of him.

"What do they do for it?" I asked, afraid of the answer.

"Nothing much. There's no cure."

"You're saying he's going to *die?*"

"Yeah. Well, I mean they say you don't die from *it* . . . you die from *complications* associated with it. But yeah, basically it's fatal."

"How long does he have?" I asked.

"They say between ten and twenty-five years. Probably closer to ten."

"Wow. I'm really sorry."

He nodded and stared straight ahead for a long time.

"Can I do anything?" I finally asked. It was a stupid question, I know, but what are you supposed to say?

He shook his head and kept staring ahead as an awkward silence began to grow. My thoughts started racing, trying to figure out what I was supposed to do.

Pray? Well, obviously I was supposed to pray. But I mean, *out loud?* That's not exactly something I usually did around Tanner. Okay, actually it wasn't something I'd *ever* done around Tanner. I'd prayed with probably hundreds of strangers, no problem. *But with Tanner?* All I could do now was sit there like a coward and scold myself as the awkward silence grew.

"It's genetic," Tanner finally said quietly.

"What?"

"I said it's *genetic*."

Tenth grade biology . . . *Punnet squares, dominant genes, probability.* Yeah. I remembered all that stuff. So, Chase must have gotten one recessive gene from their mom and one recessive gene from their dad. *But that meant there was a chance that Tanner had too . . . or Jordan.*

Now I hardly noticed the silence in Tanner's truck as my mind started calculating probabilities. There was a twenty-five percent chance that any one of them would get it and Chase was already diagnosed. So, the chance that any *two* of them would get it was only (*only?*) one in sixteen. *All three of them?* One in sixty-four.

"There's a fifty percent chance that I'll get it too," Tanner said. "Or Jordan."

"No, no, no," I assured him, glad that my superior math skills were about to make him feel somewhat better. "There's a fifty-fifty chance that you got one gene from your mom and a fifty-fifty chance that you got one from your dad. Right there, that's only a twenty-five percent chance. Then, the chances that more than one of you–"

"That's only for *recessive* genes," Tanner interrupted. "This is an autosomal dominant gene."

And that's when I realized he knew a whole lot more about it than I did.

"Autosomal dominant?" I asked.

Tanner nodded and looked at me.

"Most lethal genes *are* recessive," he agreed. "If they were dominant, whoever had them would die before they ever had a chance to pass them on."

Lethal genes . . .

"But," he went on, "Huntington's isn't like that since it doesn't usually show up until middle age or so . . . *after* people've already had kids. Chase has early onset. It doesn't usually show up this young."

"Who gave it to Chase?" I asked.

"Not sure," Tanner said. "Mom hasn't shown any symptoms yet, but that doesn't really mean anything – it can show up really late in life too. But I'm betting it was Dad. I think he found out he had it and couldn't deal with it and that's why he killed himself. Or, Danica says that a neurological disease like this can also cause psychological problems – depression and stuff – that could have made him suicidal. Either way, I'm thinking it's why he did it."

Danica was married to our good friend, Mike. He was a medical doctor. She was a psychiatrist.

6

"So Mike and Danica both know?"

"Yeah, and my mom. But nobody else needs to know right now, okay?"

"I'm not going to keep this from Laci."

"Well, obviously," he rolled his eyes.

"Does Natalie know?"

"Yeah."

"What about Jordan?"

"No way," Tanner said adamantly, shaking his head. "We're not gonna tell him – at least not until he's got his freshman year under his belt. He's got enough on his mind right now without something like this ruining college for him. We might not even tell him until he graduates, if we can keep it from him. We'll just have to see how bad Chase gets and how fast."

I sat back in my seat, trying to process everything.

"Can't they find out if you've got the gene or not?" I finally asked.

"Yeah," Tanner nodded. "They can do genetic testing."

"Are you gonna get tested?"

"I don't know," he said. "Would you wanna find out?"

I barely had a chance to think about whether I would or not before he went on.

"I mean, if I test positive, it's not like they can do anything about it. And they wouldn't be able to tell me *when* I'm going to become symptomatic. Could be next year, could be forty years from now. Why not just enjoy life and not worry about it?"

"Aren't you kinda gonna worry about it anyway?" I asked.

"Probably," he admitted. "I didn't say I wasn't going to get tested. I just said I don't know yet. I haven't really had a whole lot of time to wrap my mind around all this. It's all happened kind of fast."

I nodded and we lapsed into silence again.

My mind was swirling. Tanner (who was for all intents and purposes my best friend) was sitting here telling me that he could be dying. I found myself wondering just one thing.

Was he saved?

It was something I didn't know. Something I'd wondered and worried about for years. Something Laci and I had prayed about. But not something I'd ever actually done anything about.

Talk to him, you coward! Offer to pray with him. Make sure he knows Jesus.

"Well, anyway. I just wanted to let you know," Tanner said, breaking the silence.

"If I can do anything . . ." I said, again aware of how stupid that sounded.

"Thanks." He nodded and tried to give me a smile.

"Listen, Tanner," I said, trying to beat down the coward inside of me. "I want you to know that I'm going to be praying for you. Me and Laci, both."

"Thanks," he said again, smiling a little more successfully.

I gave him a smile back and opened my door.

"Don't forget what I said though," Tanner called as I stepped out of the car. "Jordan is *not* to find out about this right now!"

I nodded, slammed the door, and started toward the house, thinking about his last words – that he didn't want Jordan to find out.

That meant that Charlotte couldn't find out either.

~ ~ ~

WHILE LACI WAS getting the kids ready for bed that evening, I went into my office and did a quick search on Huntington's Disease.

Early symptoms may include mood swings, depression, irritability . . . involuntary facial movements . . . trouble driving, difficulty learning new things, remembering a fact, or making a decision . . . mild balance problems, clumsiness, and personality changes.

As the disease progresses, patients may have trouble feeding themselves and swallowing . . . experience sudden, jerky, and involuntary movements throughout their body, have severe problems with coordination and balance . . . hesitant, halting, or slurred speech . . . jerky, rapid eye movements . . . dementia.

The disease usually doesn't manifest itself until middle age . . . disease progression is often more severe and may progress quicker in younger patients . . . young people who develop Huntington's disease may have signs and symptoms that mimic Parkinson's disease including: muscle rigidity, tremors, and slow movements . . . seizures may also occur in those with early-onset Huntington's disease.

Death usually occurs ten to thirty years after symptoms first appeared . . . disease progression may occur faster in younger people.

After I'd brushed my teeth that night, I walked into our bedroom to find Laci sitting in bed, reading.
"You got a new Bible?" I asked.
She nodded.
"How come?"

She shrugged and looked down, but then she looked back up at me.

"I gave my other one to Tanner," she said quietly.

"You *what?*"

Her "other one" was Greg's old Bible. Mrs. White had given it to her after he'd died and I think it was Laci's most valuable possession. If the house caught fire she'd save the kids, that Bible, me, and then the dog . . . *in that order.*

"I think he . . . he needs it more than I do right now," she explained.

"So you already know?" I asked.

"Know what?"

I shook my head.

"*Why* did you give him your Bible?" I asked.

"I just . . . I just felt like he was really going through some stuff," she said, "and I thought he should have it."

"But he didn't tell you what was going on?"

She shook her head.

I sat down on the bed next to her and took one of her hands.

"It's not good," I said gently.

"What?" she asked, squeezing my hand as I saw fear flash across her face.

"Chase is really sick," I told her.

"Chase?"

"Yeah," I nodded. "Do you know anything about Huntington's disease?"

She shook her head, and so I explained it all to her . . . about the hallucinations and the swallowing and the paralysis. Then I got to the part about Tanner and Jordan each having a fifty percent chance of having it too.

"No," Laci whispered, tears welling up in her eyes.

I nodded.

"No, no, no, no, NO!" she cried, burying her head on my shoulder.

"I'm sorry," I said. I held her tight and stroked her hair while she wept. Finally, she stopped crying and sat back.

"How did Tanner seem?" she asked, wiping her eyes.

"Um, I don't know. Okay, I guess . . . all things considered."

"What about Jordan?" she wanted to know.

"Jordan doesn't know right now," I explained. "We can't let anybody know . . . especially him or Charlotte."

"But they have to find out sometime!"

"I know," I said. "But they want Jordan to get through his first year at college without having something like this on his mind."

"Jordan's a lot stronger than they're giving him credit for," Laci said.

"I know," I said. "I think they'll be surprised at how well he handles it, but right now it's not up to us."

"And how are we supposed to keep this from Charlotte?"

"Well," I said, "we won't be seeing her as much now that she's away, so that'll help . . ."

"Are you kidding?" Laci asked. "She's only two hours away. We're gonna see her all the time!"

"We're just gonna have to pretend we don't know about it," I said.

"I wish I *didn't* know about it," Laci said, tears coming into her eyes again.

"I know," I said. "Me, too."

~ ~ ~

TWO DAYS LATER, Tanner called and told me that he'd decided to get tested for Huntington's. He must have also decided that life was too short and that he was going to enjoy it no matter what, because he bought himself a new pontoon boat and was going to have a big picnic on Cross Lake.

"This weekend. Can you and Laci make it?"

"It's gonna be crowded," I warned. "It's Labor Day weekend."

"I know," he said, "but I figure if we get there early enough we can have our pick of spots, and if we don't get a good spot we'll just hang out on the boat. It's big enough."

"I'll double check with Laci," I said. "But that sounds great."

"I'm gonna ask Mike and Danica and Ashlyn and Brent. And Natalie and her new boyfriend are coming."

"Her new boyfriend!?" I cried. "I thought you were her new boyfriend!"

"Naw," he said. "We decided it wasn't gonna work out."

"Aw, Tanner . . . now I'm gonna get yelled at."

"Why are you going to get yelled at?"

"'Cause every time *you* screw up *I* get yelled at."

"I didn't screw up," he said. "It was a mutual decision."

"Yeah, I'll bet."

"It was," he insisted. "We're still friends."

"You have a *lot* of friends," I told him, shaking my head.

Charlotte found out about the picnic and – never one to pass up a day on the lake – invited herself along. Jordan, unfortunately, wasn't planning on coming home until Christmas.

"Plane tickets are *sooooo* expensive," she explained on the ride up to the lake. Tanner, Charlotte, Laci and I were riding in Tanner's truck, pulling the boat. Mike was following us with Danica, Natalie

12

and Julian – Natalie's new boyfriend. (Ashlyn and Brent hadn't been able to come.) "I'm flying down there over fall break and my ticket was over seven hundred dollars!"

"*You're spending over seven hundred dollars just to see Jordan for a couple of days?*" I exclaimed.

"About a thousand if you wanna count my hotel room and stuff."

"Is that really smart, Charlotte?" I asked. "Can't you just wait 'til he comes home at Christmas?"

"That's over *three months* away!" she cried. "I'm not waiting three months to see him!"

"Charlotte–," I began.

"Don't start, David!" she interrupted. "I'm *not* in the mood for one of your lectures about my money."

After her dad and brother had been murdered, a trust fund had been set up for Charlotte. Once Charlotte's sweet little seven-year old face had been splashed across the Internet and TV news, donations poured in and had been accumulating interest for the last ten years. I didn't know exactly how much money there was, only that (according to Mrs. White) there was enough so that she could "get her bachelor's degree *and* her master's from any university in the country and still have money left over".

When Charlotte had turned eighteen, she had legally gained access to all of that money, but then she had also received a full scholarship to State. Now – with all that money at her disposal – I just wanted to make sure that she made wise decisions.

"I don't think you need to be squandering all your money away," I told her. "One day you're going to want that money for something!"

"Guess what? I *already* want that money for something! I want it for a plane ticket to go see Jordan!"

"David," Laci interjected, "I don't think it's unreasonable for Charlotte to spend a little bit of her money."

"A thousand dollars is not a 'little bit of money'!" I protested.

"Well," Tanner argued under his breath, "relatively speaking . . ."

"Shut up, Tanner," I said. "Look, Charlotte, you start spending a little bit here and a little bit there, and pretty soon it's all gonna be gone. And what are you going to have to show for it? You need to be frugal!"

"Frugal?"

"Yes, frugal!"

"Nobody uses that word anymore, David. You sound like my mom."

Tanner grinned.

"Shut-up, Tanner," I said again.

"I didn't say anything," he laughed.

"Look, David," Laci began, but Charlotte cut her off.

"No, no, Laci. He's right. I need to be more *frugal*. I'll cancel my hotel reservation and just shack up with Jordan in his dorm room. That'll save about three hundred bucks."

"Very funny, Charlotte," I said, and Tanner and Laci both laughed.

"I'm just trying to be frugal!"

"Guess what?" Laci asked, successfully changing the subject. "I might be flying to Texas myself in December."

"What?" I asked, craning my neck to see her because she was sitting behind me.

"Yeah," she nodded. "I haven't had a chance to tell you yet, but I've been invited to speak to Ergon's Board of Directors."

Ergon was Ergon Ministries – the organization that Laci had worked for when we'd lived in Mexico. Its name came from the Greek word for "work" – as it's used in Colossians 1:10 – *bearing fruit in every good work*. Ergon Ministries was an outreach program, specializing in providing organized mission trips for youth groups from the US After the groups raised enough money, they could work at an orphanage (the same one we'd adopted our children Dorito and Lily from) and at a landfill where the poorest of the poor lived.

"Whoa, whoa, whoa," I said. "You're not going back to work for them."

I meant it as a question, but it came out as a statement.

14

"I didn't say I was going back to work for them," she answered evenly. "They just asked me if I could fly down there for this one event."

"How long would you be gone?"

"I don't know. Probably four days."

"Four days?! What am I supposed to do while you're gone for four days?"

"I'm confident you can handle it," she said, patting me on the arm.

"What about the kids?"

"I'm confident you can handle that, too."

"I can't believe you're gonna leave the kids for four days!"

"You just told me that I needed some time away from them!" she exclaimed. "Remember? That's why they're with your parents right now instead of with us!"

She deepened her voice to imitate me. "Let's get my parents to watch 'em, Laci. You need time away from the kids."

"One little picnic is a whole lot different than four days!"

"I'll come over and check on him," Tanner promised Laci.

"Thank you," she answered.

"When is it?" Charlotte asked.

"Well, I'd probably fly out on the fifteenth and fly back on the eighteenth."

"I'll be coming home for Christmas break on the sixteenth," Charlotte said. "I'll check on him too."

"See?" Laci asked me. "You'll be fine. You'll hardly even know I'm gone."

"I couldn't believe it when Tanner told me that you and Danica were actually going to join us," I told Mike while we were waiting for Tanner to back the boat trailer onto the ramp.

"I couldn't believe that somebody called me and wanted something other than free medical advice," Mike answered.

15

"Actually, now that you mention it, my shoulder's been aching," I told him, rubbing it.

"I'll be glad to amputate."

"How's your mom?" Laci asked him.

"You'll never guess," he answered.

"She's getting married!" Laci squealed. (Mike's dad had died the summer before Mike started high school.)

"Okay," Mike muttered, "maybe you *can* guess."

"Really?" I asked. Mike nodded.

"Do you, I mean . . . is he a nice guy?"

Mike shrugged. "I guess."

Just then Tanner hopped out of his truck and looked at us.

"All right, which one of you clowns is driving?"

"Driving the boat or the truck?" I asked.

"I shudder at the thought of either," he said, "but since I can't clone myself . . ."

"I'll drive the boat," I volunteered.

"Good choice."

"Shut up, Tanner."

A few years earlier, I'd turned too sharply while backing the boat into his garage and the boat trailer had put a hole in his tailgate.

Mike jumped up into the boat with me and Tanner stood on the wheel-well, leaning over the side.

"Don't touch anything else!" he growled after he was finished showing us how to start it and back it off the trailer. "I don't even know what half these buttons do."

"We're a doctor and an engineer," Mike pointed out. "I think we can handle it."

"Don't touch anything else," he warned again. He patted the boat. "I'm sorry, girl."

"He's not sorry," I told the boat. "He's clearly choosing the truck over you."

16

Cross Lake was dotted with islands and, like Tanner had suspected, we'd arrived at the lake early enough to find one without a crowd. He beached the pontoon boat and he and Mike started cleaning out a fire pit we found about twenty feet from the shore. Charlotte was on the phone with Jordan. Natalie and Julian headed off down the beach in one direction, looking for wood, and Laci and I went in the other.

Before long, we came across a little creek, filled with cold water and covered with a blanket of tiny algae. Frog eyes disappeared beneath the surface as we approached, and when we got very close, several of them leaped to safety.

"Dorito and Lily would love this," Laci said. "We'll have to remember this place next time we come here."

"See?" I said. "You can't stop thinking about the kids. How are you gonna survive without them for four days?"

"If you don't want me to go, I won't," she said.

I sighed. "What do they want? Why are you going?"

"They were thinking about starting a campaign to expand the ministry before I left, but now they're having trouble just keeping things going like they were. Aaron wants me to talk to the board and help them redefine the search parameters and pay scale and everything."

Aaron was her old boss, and apparently he hadn't been able to find a suitable replacement for Laci since she'd left two years earlier.

"You're irreplaceable," I told her. I got only a small smile from her.

"Look," I said, "you know I don't care if you want to go to Texas for four days, but . . ."

"You're worried they're going to try to convince me to go back?"

"Yes."

"David," she said, stopping and taking my hand. "You know I wouldn't go back there unless God lets us know that's what He wants us to do."

I leaned my forehead against hers and held both of her hands.

"I don't want to go back there," I told her.

"I know you don't."

"I do *not* want to go back!"

"I know," she said again, squeezing my hands, "but you will if God tells us to, right?"

"You know I will," I said unhappily.

"So then, let's quit worrying about it right now. I don't think that's what this is about. This is just about them getting some practical feedback from me. It's a one-time thing."

Somehow I doubted that, but I nodded, and we started walking into the woods.

"So, when do you go?" I asked, leaning down and picking up a large tree limb.

"They want me to fly down there on Tuesday the fifteenth and then I'd come home on Friday. That's the last day of school for Dorito before Christmas break."

"So that's really only three nights," I said, breaking the limb in half over my knee. "I guess I could have dinner with my mom and dad one night and with your parents one night and with Mrs. White one night . . ."

"You think you'll be able to make it?" she smiled.

"Yeah," I said. "I'll be fine."

After lunch we all went swimming and then Laci and I spread a blanket out on the beach and lay down to dry off in the sun. Charlotte helped Mike spread out another blanket and they both sat down on it.

"So tell us about this guy your mom's marrying," Charlotte suggested.

"I dunno," Mike said, shrugging.

"You don't seem too thrilled about him," Laci noted.

"It's not *him*," Mike said. "I think that no matter who it was I'd probably be a bit . . ."

18

"Overprotective?" Laci guessed.

"I suppose," he admitted.

"My mom dated some guy when I was in middle school."

"Mr. Barnett?" Mike asked.

"Yeah," Charlotte nodded. "I hated him."

"Why?" Mike asked.

"I think mostly because I was in middle school," she smiled. "It's like you said, there wasn't really anything wrong with *him* . . ."

"She hasn't dated anyone since then, has she?" he asked.

"No," Charlotte said, "and now I really wish she'd find somebody. I'm not there very much anymore and I hate her being all alone . . ."

Mike sighed.

"When's the wedding?" I asked.

"I don't know," Mike said. "They just got engaged."

"How long have they known each other?" Laci wanted to know.

"I guess ever since we moved. He goes to our church."

"What's he do for a living?" Charlotte asked.

This went on for a while as we continued to grill Mike for details about his future step-father. Ultimately, we decided that his mom could do worse.

"I suppose," Mike finally agreed.

I rolled over onto my back and sat up on my elbows.

"What's up with those two?" I asked, pointing at the pontoon boat where Natalie and Tanner were deep in conversation.

"What about 'em?" Charlotte asked.

"Don't you think it's odd that Natalie brought her new boyfriend along, but she's spending all her time with Tanner?"

"Maybe she's keeping her options open," Charlotte laughed.

"And what about them?" I asked Mike, pointing offshore about ten yards. Danica and Julian were still in the water and seemed to be engrossed in a discussion of their own. "Isn't that *your* wife?"

"Ah," Mike said. "That one I can explain. Julian's a counselor. He's probably still picking Danica's brain. They talked about the Oedipus complex the entire ride up here."

"The *what?*" I asked.

"Never mind," he said. "You don't want to know."

"Well," I said, rolling over and wrapping my arm around Laci. "You'll notice that *my* significant other is right here by my side."

"Actually," she said, "I was just going to see if Mike wanted to take a stroll with me down the shore."

"Ha, ha, ha," I said as she kissed me.

"I miss Jordan!" Charlotte wailed.

"When's he coming home?" Mike asked her.

"Not until Christmas."

"That's a long time," he acknowledged.

"Oh, but don't worry," I said. "She's going down there over fall break."

"That'll be fun," Mike said.

"I'm hitchhiking," she told Mike.

"You are not."

"Yes, I am," she said as her phone rang. "And I'm shacking up with him when I get there. I'm going to be *frugal.*"

She stood up as she answered her phone and started heading down the beach.

"Talking about you," we heard her say as she walked away.

"So neither one of them have any clue about Chase?" Mike asked as soon as she was out of earshot.

"No," I said. Mike shook his head.

"I don't see how they're gonna keep this from Jordan for almost a year. From what Tanner's told me, Chase is already quite symptomatic."

"I think they're just going to come up with reasons why Chase can never make it home at the same time Jordan's home. Jordan's only coming home for Christmas break and maybe Easter break . . ."

"You know how mad Charlotte's gonna be when she finds out that we all knew and didn't tell her?" Mike asked.

"I know," I sighed. "I'm dreading it."

"Did you know that Tanner's decided to get tested?" Laci asked Mike.

20

"Yeah," he answered. "I talked to him about it. I actually recommended the genetic testing company he's gonna use."

"Why can't he just go to his doctor?"

"He can, but then that information becomes part of his medical record. There are so many direct-to-consumer genetic testing companies available nowadays, I think it's safer for him to go that route."

"Safer?" I asked.

"Let's say he's got it," Mike said and Laci winced, "and his insurance company finds out about it. What do you think they're gonna do?"

"They can't drop him, can they?"

"No, not legally," Mike said, "but I think they'd be looking for any loophole they could find so that they could legally drop him. Plus, you're talking about the fact that he may not become symptomatic for years . . . I mean like twenty, thirty, forty years. There's a very good chance that he might want to change jobs or something before he ever even gets sick. What insurance company do you think is gonna accept him?"

Mike shook his head. "I just think he'd be better off sitting on that information. I don't think he should take the chance of having something like that in his records."

"Well, is that *ethical?*" I asked. "I mean . . . if he knows he's got it and he doesn't tell them?"

"I don't know," Mike muttered. "I personally don't think I'd get tested."

"Really?"

"I don't know," he said. "I guess it's gonna be hard, either way."

"Unless the test comes back negative," Laci said.

"Right," Mike agreed.

"How long before he finds out?" Laci asked.

"He's probably not gonna find out until close to Thanksgiving."

"*Thanksgiving?*" I exclaimed. "Why so long?"

"Well, after he gets his blood drawn, it'll take about four to six weeks for the results to come back, but the company that he's using won't even test him until he's undergone some counseling."

"Counseling?"

"Yeah," he nodded, "They counsel him first before they even decide if they're gonna test him or not. You know, make sure he's not gonna commit suicide or something if he finds out it's positive, make sure he agrees to continue with counseling if it is . . ."

"I *hate* this," Laci said, putting her hands over her eyes. "I hate it, I hate it, I HATE it!"

"Hate what?" I heard Charlotte's voice ask.

We all turned and saw that she was back.

"This sunscreen," Laci said without missing a beat. "I got some in my eyes."

"You're done talking to Jordan already?" I asked.

"I'm gonna call him back in a little bit," she said, throwing her phone down onto the blanket and stripping down to her bathing suit. "I'm gonna go check on your wife," she told Mike. "Find out what they're *really* talking about."

"Good to know you've got my back," Mike smiled at her as she headed toward the water. Then he turned to Laci.

"Man, you're a good liar," he whispered.

"She always has been," I said wryly.

"And this doesn't worry you?" he asked with a smile.

"As far as I know," I said, "she only uses her powers for good."

"I don't know," he said. "I think I'd be a bit concerned if my wife could think up lies that fast."

"What you need to be concerned about is the fact that your wife is out there in the water having a big ol' conversation with some good-looking guy."

"Charlotte will take care of things for me," he said, nodding toward them. Then he looked at me and asked worriedly, "You really think he's good-looking?"

"He's better looking than you!"

"Oh, he is not!" Laci protested, swatting me.

22

"You don't think he's good looking?" I asked her, doubtfully.

"I think he's good-looking," she admitted. "But he's not better looking than Mike."

"Is he better looking than me?" I wanted to know.

"Of course not," she smiled, patting my hand.

"Man," Mike said, looking at her again and shaking his head. "I really can't *believe* how good you lie!"

~ ~ ~

NEITHER ONE OF us had to lie to Charlotte too much during the fall. She came home almost every weekend and we almost always had her and her mom over for dinner or went over there when she was home, but fortunately, the conversation never worked its way around to Chase. She flew to Texas during the third week in October, a few weeks after Tanner finished his counseling and had his blood drawn. As Halloween drew near, we found ourselves firmly entrenched in regular routines.

Dorito – in the second grade now – loved school. His teacher's name was Mrs. Spell (I'm not making that up – that really was her name.) and he loved her too. He was also old enough to finally enroll in Cub Scouts and couldn't wait to enter his first official Pinewood Derby race. Last year, they'd allowed the Tiger Cubs to have their own race, but he'd known it wasn't "the real thing" and he was already planning out what his car was going to look like this year.

Lily was almost three. Born completely deaf, Lily had received cochlear implants a year and a half earlier that had allowed her to finally hear. She went regularly to a speech therapist and Laci worked with her daily. Verbally, she had almost caught up with her peers, although she was still a pretty quiet kid (especially compared to Dorito).

Laci enrolled Lily in a Mother's Morning Out program at church and every Friday had a few hours to herself. The first day she had spent her free time in the parking lot with her cell phone gripped in her hand, ready to bolt to Lily's rescue, but after seeing how well Lily did, Laci began using her time to visit with her mom or her friends. Usually I picked Lily up on Fridays so that Laci could go out for lunch. She also went to choir practice every Wednesday night.

I still worked out of my home as a structural engineer, so I pretty much set my own schedule. I was a den leader in Dorito's pack, and I also led a youth group. Two years earlier I had gotten roped into leading the one at Jordan's church and I was still doing that, even

24

though I really wanted to get out of it. I also wanted to quit attending church there and go back to the one we'd grown up in, but Laci felt that they needed us and she didn't think we should leave.

All in all, things were pretty good. Of course I worried about Huntington's disease, and I worried that Laci might suddenly "get the call" from God for us to go back to Mexico. But overall, I was pretty happy.

The first day of November fell on a Monday – the day of the week that Tanner and I usually tried to play racquetball. I had a bunch of pictures on my phone of the kids in their Halloween costumes and I showed them to him before we left the locker room. After he'd seen them all I asked him about his test results.

"You still haven't heard anything?" I said as I slipped my phone into my jacket pocket and put it into my locker.

"No," he answered, closing his locker. "I told you, I'll tell you as soon as I hear something."

"I just don't see what could possibly take so long," I said as we headed toward the court.

"They said four to six weeks," he reminded me.

"How long's it been?"

"Three and a half."

I sighed.

"Cheer up," he said. "Maybe if I get sick you'll finally be able to beat me!"

"I've beaten you before!" I protested.

"Maybe once."

"Twice!" I said.

"I was probably sick then, too," he said, opening the door to the court.

"I don't think so," I said. "But, anyway, I'd much rather have your test come back negative and keep getting beat."

"Me, too," he replied, turning serious, "but you know what I'm gonna do if it's positive?"

"What?" I asked, pulling my goggles down over my eyes.

"I'm gonna get into some kind of clinical trial."

"Really?"

"Yeah," he said. "I've already been looking into it and there's all sorts of research going on."

"Does any of it look promising?" I asked.

"I don't know," he shrugged. "I think they tend to put more of a positive spin on things than there really is, but, you know, I could maybe help them learn more about it. Do somebody else some good down the road."

I nodded.

"Who knows," he said, pulling his goggles on. "Maybe that's why I'm here."

"Huh?"

"You know. Maybe that's what I was put on this earth for. Maybe that's my purpose in life. I might have to go through this, but one day somebody else's life will be better because of me. Know what I mean?"

You were put on this earth to worship God. Your purpose is to love Him.

Naturally, all I could do was nod at him.

"Ready to get whooped?" he asked.

I nodded again.

We played our usual three games and (of course) he beat me soundly each time. I was mad at myself for (once again) being gutless when it came to talking to Tanner about my faith, but by the time we got back to the locker room, I'd figured out what I wanted to say to him. Unfortunately, I never got the chance.

I could hear my phone beeping as I got near my locker, letting me know that I had a text. I pulled it out and saw that it was a message from my boss, Scott. He hardly ever called me in the evening, and it was even more rare for him to send a text.

Call me.

"I gotta see what this is about," I told Tanner, hitting send.

"What's up?" I asked when Scott answered.

"Have you been watching the news?" he asked.

"No. Why? What's going on?"

"It's the Terrarium, Dave. It's not good."

The Terrarium in downtown Phoenix was one of the first projects that I'd been the lead engineer on. It was really called the Patterson Span and was an S-shaped, glass-covered walkway that connected the third floor of one building with the fourth floor of another building diagonally across the street. The fact that we'd had to overcome its tendency to heat up like a parked car with the windows rolled up in the summertime had earned it the nickname "The Terrarium."

There was a TV in the locker room, but it was off. I stepped over to it and turned it on, flipping the channel as Scott filled me in on what had happened.

Between Scott and CNN, it wasn't long before I had all of the facts. The whole thing had collapsed onto the street below. *Three people confirmed dead, dozens of others injured . . . some critically. Rescue workers were still searching the rubble, looking for survivors. No word yet on the cause.*

~ ~ ~

SCOTT ASSURED ME that everyone was behind me and they were confident I'd done nothing wrong. All the same, company policy was that I be suspended – with pay – pending an investigation.

And apparently it was a *criminal* investigation because the next day I was served with a search warrant and my computer was confiscated along with all the blueprints and files from the project.

I went over to Tanner's that afternoon and used his computer to pull up my old emails.

"Aren't they blocking access to your account?" Tanner asked me.

"I set up a new account in Laci's name and forwarded everything to it yesterday."

"Isn't that illegal?" he wanted to know.

"I didn't *change* anything," I told him. "I just wanted to make sure I had copies of everything."

"Well," he said, looking at me doubtfully, "I hope you don't take me down with you."

I saved everything onto an external hard drive and spent hours poring over every attachment and correspondence I could find, searching for any hint of error ... any mistake I might have made that could have caused the collapse. I found nothing.

But, according to the news that emerged in the days after the collapse, there was no evidence of a bomb or any other type of terrorist activity. No signs that there'd been an earthquake or that anything had hit it or disturbed it in any way. And there'd only been about seventy-five people on it ... well under the three hundred person limit it had been designed for.

Everything was pointing to some sort of structural problem and independent teams were being sent to inspect all other bridges and walkways that our company had worked on.

28

Scott called again two days after the collapse.

"The girders . . . the cables . . . corroded beyond belief," he said.

"Corroded?"

"I've seen seventy-year-old bridges with less rust."

Corroded.

"What caused it?" I asked.

"It's probably gonna be a while before we know for sure. I'll keep you posted."

"Thanks."

I went back over to Tanner's and let myself in. This time I focused on the materials: the steel support girders, the cable composition, the concrete. Tanner got home from work and found me almost smiling.

"Good news?" he asked.

"Not bad news," I answered. Everything had been done by the book. All the materials and specifications we'd mandated were industry standard.

"Somebody might have substituted inferior products or something," I explained to Tanner, "but if they did, then they did it against our direction."

"But what if you designed it wrong?" he hesitated. "Like, what if water dripped down in there where it wasn't supposed to go and rusted it out or something?"

"Stick to football, buddy," I said confidently. "This was not my fault."

"Well, good," he nodded, walking to his pantry. "Wanna hear some more good news?"

"What?" I asked.

He leaned in for some peanuts and glanced at me with a smile before he popped the can open. "I got my results back."

~ ~ ~

"YOU KNOW WHAT you should do until this is all over?" Laci asked me that night after we'd turned out the lights. Even though I was pretty confident I was going to be cleared of any wrongdoing and fully reinstated, there was the possibility that it would be weeks before that happened.

"What?"

"You should go volunteer in Dorito's classroom. Take advantage of this time you've got. Dorito would *love* to have you in there."

"And do *what?*" I asked.

"I don't know," I felt her shrug. "They sent home something at the beginning of the year asking for volunteers. I didn't sign up for anything because of Lily, but I know they could use some help."

"I don't know . . ." I hesitated.

"I bet you could teach 'em *math*."

"Really?"

"Oh, sure," she said sarcastically. "I bet you could, like, institute some big *geometry* project or something . . . maybe you could teach them all to use *graphing calculators!* Ooh! That would be fun, wouldn't it?"

"Geometry is just *shapes*, Laci, and graphing calculators really aren't that hard . . ."

"Just remember that they're only in the second grade, okay?" she sighed.

"Okay," I said, "I'll try to keep it in mind."

Thursday I took Dorito to school, walked him in, and talked to his teacher, Mrs. Spell, about volunteering. She told me that what they needed most was for someone to work daily with one small group of students who were "struggling a bit" with their reading and writing.

30

"I'm more of a math person," I told her.

"Can you read and write?" she asked.

I nodded.

"You'll be fine," she assured me. "Would you like to start tomorrow morning, or do you want to wait until Monday?"

"I can start today if you want," I said.

"I'm going to have to rearrange their reading groups a little bit first," she said. "Let's start tomorrow."

"Okay," I said. "See you tomorrow."

Dorito was bouncing off the walls when he found out that I was going to be taking him to school every day and working in his classroom.

"You can meet Amber," he gushed. "She's one of my best friends!"

Amber, it turned out, was in the small group I was assigned to. There were four kids in the group: Amber, Mariah, Drake, and Christian. My first morning there, Mrs. Spell sat all of them down around a circular table and introduced them to me and told them what we were going to be doing.

My first task was to have the kids dictate a story for me to type out on the computer. Then I'd print it out and staple it together and let them illustrate it.

"Reading stories they've written really helps to increase their reading skills," Mrs. Spell had explained.

The others were supposed to read silently while they were waiting for me, so I told them to take out their books.

"I thought you said these kids were struggling?" I asked Mrs. Spell when I saw Amber pull a Harry Potter book out of her desk. I wasn't a huge fan or anything, but I knew enough about Harry Potter to know that it wasn't typical second grade reading fare.

"She's not really reading it," Mrs. Spell said quietly.

"Really?"

31

"No. She can't read or write at all. She's just pretending," Mrs. Spell said, heading over to another table. "You'll see."

I sat down in front of the computer with Mariah.

"All right, Mariah," I said. "I want you to tell me a story and I'm going to type what you say. Okay?"

She nodded.

"Once upon a time," Mariah began, "there was a pretty fairy. She lived at the beach inside of a seashell. One day a crab crawled into her shell and scared her so she flew away. The end."

"That's all you want to say?" I asked.

She nodded.

"Are you sure? That's kind of a short book."

"I'm sure."

"Okay," I hesitated. "I guess we can put one sentence on each page, and then you can draw a lot of pictures."

In a few minutes I had Mariah's ready and I called Amber over to the computer.

"I wanna be next," Christian whined.

"Ladies first," I told him, and then I smiled at Amber.

The first thing I noticed about Amber was that she had a rat's nest in the back of her hair. How could anyone send a kid to school with a huge knot like that in their hair? I honestly didn't see how anyone was ever going to get that mess untangled. She sat down in the chair next to me.

That's when I noticed a second thing about her.

She *stank*. Or was that stunk? (Maybe I shouldn't have been helping the kids with their writing after all . . .)

"Hi, Amber," I said. "I want you to tell me a story, okay?"

She blinked at me.

What was that smell? Stale cigarettes?

"You just tell me what you want to say and I'll type it for you . . . what do you want me to type?"

Second graders couldn't have body odor, could they?

Amber didn't say anything.

"She don't talk," Mariah informed me.

32

Cat urine?

"She *doesn't* talk," I corrected.

"That's what I said."

I sighed.

"What do you mean?" I asked Mariah.

"I mean she don't talk. She don't never say nothin'." I let the triple negative slide.

I looked at Amber and took a deep breath (through my mouth). I smiled at her, but she didn't smile back. Instead, she folded her hands onto her lap and then looked away, staring at the blank computer screen.

I finished Christian's story and told Drake we'd start on his first thing the next day. Then I found Mrs. Spell.

"Does Amber ever talk?" I asked her.

"No."

"How can she *not* talk? What's wrong with her?"

"I can't really get into specifics like that about a student."

"Well . . . how am I supposed to work with her?"

"I know it's hard," Mrs. Spell acknowledged. "Just do what you can. I'm not expecting any miracles."

~ ~ ~

"HEY, DORITO?" I asked that night at dinner. "You said yesterday that you and Amber are friends?"

"Yep," he nodded, taking a big spoonful of applesauce.

"Do you two play together?"

"Yeah."

"Really?"

"Yeah. I play with her all the time."

"What kinds of things do you two play?"

"Wolf."

"Wolf?"

"Yep," he nodded.

"And how exactly do you play that?"

"Well," he said, "we make a nest in the mulch under the slide, and we catch tigers and stuff and feed them to our babies."

"Uh-huh. And do you talk to her?"

"Sure."

That was a *dumb* question.

"Does she talk to you?"

"Yeah."

"Really?"

"Uh-huh."

"Tell me something she says to you."

"Umm," he thought for a minute and then he rubbed his hand on his stomach . . . the sign for "hungry".

"Oh!" I said. "She *signs?*"

"Uh-huh," he said again, nodding. "I taught her how."

The following Monday I knocked out Drake's story in about ten minutes and then I called Amber over. She laid down her Harry

Potter book and walked to me and sat down. Nothing had improved in the hair or body odor department.

"Hi, Amber!" I said. "You know I'm Dorito's dad, right?"

She nodded.

"He says you guys play together."

She nodded again.

"He says you use sign language sometimes?"

She nodded one more time.

"Well, you know what? I know sign language too! I thought maybe we could sign together. You wanna do that?"

Okay, she signed.

"Great!" I smiled. "Will you show me some of the words you already know?"

She nodded and slowly started signing: *wolf, tiger, ice cream, puppy, baby, love, thirsty, hungry, water.*

"That's GREAT, Amber! Do you know anything else?"

She bit her lip and thought for a moment. Then she shook her head, *no*.

"Do you want to learn some more?" I asked and she nodded.

"Okay," I said. "Well, here's what I think we should do. I think we should make up a story, and I'll teach you how to sign the words in the story. Then you can read it to me using sign language. Does that sound okay?"

Okay.

"All right," I said, turning to the keyboard. "Let me think here for a second."

I started typing.

Once upon a time there were five little puppies.

She pointed at the words. Then she signed *puppy*.

"You can read that?" I asked her.

She nodded.

I typed again.

Touch your nose.

"Can you read that?" I asked her.
Nod.
"Do it," I said.
She touched her nose.

Stand up and touch your elbow.

"Do that."
She did it.
"Wow! You read great, Amber," I said. "Can you write?"
She shrugged. I handed her a pencil and paper.
"Try to write something," I suggested. "Write your name."
She gripped her pencil tightly and bit her lip. She didn't write anything.
"It's okay," I said. "Do you know what your name starts with?"
She nodded.
"It's a *B*, right?"
She shook her head at me.
"Is it an *A*?"
Nod.
"Can you make an *A*?
Shrug.
"Can you try?"
She gripped the pencil tight again and made a tiny line on her paper. Then she erased it and looked dejected.
"It's okay, Amber," I assured her. "Can you find it on the computer?"
She nodded eagerly.
"Show me."
She typed.

a . . . m . . . b . . . e . . . r

"That's GREAT!" I said. "Type something else."

She turned her body to the computer and began punching away at the keyboard. I watched – amazed – as the words slowly formed.

each puppy had a name and a specal coller from its mommy the puppy with the red coller was name coten and the puppy with the blue coller was name razebery and the puppy with the yello coller was name sunny and the puppy with the green coller was name doreto and the last puppy was amber.

"What color was Amber's collar?" I asked her.

She thought for a moment and then she typed:

purpel

I couldn't wait to tell Mrs. Spell, but she was less enthusiastic than I'd imagined she would be.

"I see," she said when I showed her the paper I'd printed out.

"Isn't this a big deal?" I asked. "I mean . . . she can *read* and she can *write*!"

"Well," she said, "it's a start, but I don't think you need to be getting your hopes up too much."

I must have looked dismayed.

"I mean . . . don't get me wrong . . . you've made more progress with her in two days than anyone else has all year, but . . ."

"But what?"

"She's a long way from reading and writing at the independent level we'd expect at this age."

"*She* wrote this!" I said, waving the paper at her. Mrs. Spell looked at me skeptically.

"You think I don't know how to spell purple?" I asked her.

"I'm sure you know how to spell purple, but–"

"Come watch, okay? Come watch what she can do."

She said something to Ms. Amy, her teaching assistant.

"All right, everyone," Ms. Amy called out to the class. "Let's all get on the carpet for a story before we go out to recess."

"Not you, Amber," Mrs. Spell said. "Would you come over to the computer for a minute?"

Amber nodded and the three of us walked over to the computer.

I typed onto the computer:

Touch your nose.

Amber looked at me, then over her shoulder at Mrs. Spell, then she folded her hands in her lap and looked down at them.

"It's okay, Amber," I assured her. "Do it."

She didn't move.

"Amber, what's wrong? Touch your nose."

She touched her nose.

"See?" I said.

"You told her to do it," Mrs. Spell said.

"I know, but . . . she can read. You can read, can't you, Amber?"

Amber shrugged at me.

I glanced up at Mrs. Spell who looked at me doubtfully.

"Amber," I said, desperately, "type something. Come on. Type some more of your story."

She looked at me uncertainly.

"It's okay. Go ahead and type."

She put her hands on the keyboard and typed:

hfidkfkjkl;p;ffnmmnt

"That's good, Amber," Mrs. Spell said, patting her on the shoulder.

"Don't be discouraged," Mrs. Spell said quietly to me. "She's doing great."

Then she gave me a look that defied me to say anything else about it. I gave her a little nod and she walked away.

I glanced back at Amber who was looking down at her hands in her lap again.

"Amber," I said. She refused to look up.

38

"It's okay, Amber," I said. "You don't have to show Mrs. Spell."

She lifted her head uncertainly and looked as if she might burst into tears at any minute.

"No, no, no," I said. "Don't cry. It'll be our secret, okay? We don't ever have to tell anyone else . . . I promise. Okay?"

She nodded and looked a little less like she was going to cry.

"Wanna go sit on the rug with me and hear the story?"

She nodded again, and we went to join story time.

"Maybe she can talk, too," Laci suggested at lunchtime when I told her everything that had happened.

"What?"

"Maybe she can talk, too. She only reads and types when she wants to, so maybe she only talks when she wants to."

"You really think so?"

"Maybe, I mean . . . why would she *not* be able to talk? I've never heard of someone's voice box not working, unless they've had like cancer or something, right?"

"How can I find out if she can talk?"

"Simple," she said. "Ask Dorito."

I picked Dorito up after school.

"Where's Mommy?" he wanted to know.

"Oh," I said casually. "I just thought I'd pick you up for a change."

"Okay."

"How was school?"

"Good."

"Good. Anything exciting happen?" I asked.

"Christian killed all our fish."

"Oh, really? How'd that happen?"

"He pumped a bunch of soap into the fish tank."

"That was mean."

"There were a lot of bubbles."

"I'll bet," I said. "Did he get in trouble?"

"No."

"Why not?!"

"Because the teacher doesn't know who did it."

"But you do?"

"Yeah."

"How do you know?"

"I just know."

"Well, did you tell the teacher?" I asked.

"No."

"Why not?"

"You're not supposed to tattletale."

I wasn't quite sure what to say to that, so I decided to move on.

"Hey, Dorito?"

"What?"

"Does Amber ever talk?"

"No."

"Not even to you?"

"No."

"Oh."

"Why?" he asked.

"I was just wondering."

After dinner that evening, I called Mike.

"What's up, Dave?"

"Am I catching you at a bad time?"

"Actually, I'm on a date with my lovely wife."

"Oh," I said. "Sorry. I'll call you back later."

"No, don't worry about it. What's going on?"

"Well," I said, "there's this little girl in Dorito's class and she doesn't ever talk – I mean, I think she's mute – and I was wondering what would cause that."

"And here I thought you were calling to invite me to go pheasant hunting or something," Mike said, "but NO, once again you're just using me for free medical advice."

"I'm sorry. I'm a terrible friend."

"Yes, you are," he agreed. "I could charge you, and then you'd just be a terrible patient . . ."

"Deal."

"Do you know anything about her?"

"Other than the fact that she stinks? No."

"She stinks?"

"Yes."

He paused. "Okay," he finally said, "we'll come back to that later. Have you seen any scars or evidence of surgery or trauma around her throat or mouth?"

"No."

"Have you heard her make any sounds? Has she laughed or giggled or anything like that?"

"I haven't even seen her smile."

"Here, you'd better talk with Danica," he said. "This sounds more like something up her alley."

"Okay."

"I should warn you, though," he said. "She charges even more than I do."

"I really do want to go pheasant hunting sometime . . ."

"Uh-huh."

"Thanks, Mike."

I heard him fill Danica in on what I'd told him before he handed the phone to her.

"So apparently she's mute?" Danica asked.

"I guess so. What would cause that?"

"Well, sometimes people are mute because something is wrong with their larynx or their larynx has been removed, but with children, that's not usually what's going on. With children it's usually an emotional inability to talk."

"What do you mean?"

"I mean there's no physical reason for it, but mentally . . . something's keeping her from speaking. Does she talk at all? Ever?"

"I'm not sure," I said. "Dorito's never heard her talk."

"Has she had the capability before, but now she's lost it?"

"I don't know."

"Can you tell if she seems to have normal intelligence?"

"Yes," I said. "I think she's smart. Dorito's been teaching her sign language and I think she's reading way above grade level and she can type. I can't get her to write, though."

"Well, without examining her or knowing *something* further about her background, anything I suggest is purely conjecture . . ."

"I know," I said, "but, like, if you had to take a guess, what would you say?"

"Okay, well, we can rule out akenetic mutism, which is good, because that's much more severe. I'd say it's probably one of two things. If she's not talking at all, I'd say it's trauma-induced mutism. If she talks in some instances and not others, then we're looking at selective mutism. But, no matter what it is, you need to understand that she's probably suffering from a psychiatric disorder. She's not simply choosing not to talk."

"Trauma-induced mutism is caused by trauma?" I guessed.

"Generally," she laughed.

"What about selective mutism?"

"It's different from trauma-induced mutism. In trauma-induced mutism, usually the subject suddenly becomes completely silent in all situations, usually as the result of some type of psychological trauma. With selective mutism, the subject is capable of speech in certain situations. For instance, she may be silent at school but talk at home. Selective mutism isn't necessarily the result of trauma, but of course that can't be ruled out."

"Do you think she'll grow out of it?"

42

"Probably not without intervention," Danica said. "Selective mutism can progress to the point where the subject won't speak anywhere and trauma-induced mutism rarely resolves itself without intervention. In both cases, early treatment is very important. Is she under the care of a psychiatrist or psychologist?"

"I don't know."

"Well, hopefully she is, but I will say it's good that she types and signs. Keep encouraging her to do that. Emailing, texting, things like that are good too. Any way you can get her to communicate with you will help her to become mentally prepared for more direct communication."

"Okay."

"And let me know if you get any more information on her and I'll see what I can tell you."

"Thanks, Danica. I really appreciate it."

"You're welcome."

"Tell Mike I'll call him about pheasant hunting."

"Yeah," Danica laughed. "Like he's got time to go pheasant hunting."

"Hi, Amber," I said when she came up to the computer on Tuesday morning.

She looked at me uncertainly.

"You wanna work on your story some more?" I asked.

Okay.

"The first thing we're gonna do is go over what you wrote yesterday, and then you can write some more, okay?"

Okay.

I showed her how to move the cursor with the mouse and put it on the first word in the story.

"Here's the sign for *little*," I said, holding my hands about a foot apart and then bringing them close together, almost as if I were clapping. "We're gonna use that for lower case letters, and here's the

43

sign for *big*." I moved my hands apart from one another. "We're gonna use that for upper case letters. Every time you start a sentence, what kind of letter do you have to use?"

Big.

"Exactly, so we have to get rid of that little *e* and make it a capital *E*. Put the cursor right after the *e* in 'each'."

She did it.

"Now, hit this button right here," I said, pointing to the backspace key.

"Excellent," I said. "Now to make a capital *E*, you hold this shift key down before you hit the *E* button, okay?"

I showed her what to do and then let her do it.

"Great," I said. "Now, every sentence has to start with a capital letter, so where else do you need to fix it?"

She pointed at the first word of the next sentence.

"That's right," I nodded. "Can you fix it by yourself?"

She nodded and fixed it. Then, she looked around the room to see where Mrs. Spell was.

"Nobody's watching," I told her, and she started typing.

"Okay, good," I said when she'd finished capitalizing all the letters at the beginning of each sentence. "Now, every time you write somebody's name, you need to use a capital letter too, so let's fix all these names."

She nodded and got to work, biting her lip in concentration. Then we fixed all the misspelled words and I taught her some new signs as we were going along.

"Do you wanna quit?" I asked her.

No.

"You wanna add some new stuff now?"

Yes.

"Okay . . . go ahead and start and I'll stop you if you spell something wrong."

She typed away, fixing *foresst* and *mowse* when I told her to. Mrs. Spell wandered by and stood behind Amber for a moment as she typed:

44

"It's 'l- e-*a*-s-h'," I told her. She fixed it.

"That's very good, Amber," Mrs. Spell said, not hiding the surprise in her voice. I winced as Amber dropped her hands into her lap.

"You wanna have the leash be in a cave?" I asked her quickly. She glanced at me as I pulled the keyboard in front of me and started typing. Mrs. Spell stood there for another moment and then walked away.

"She's gone," I told Amber, erasing what I'd written. "Now keep going."

~ ~ ~

ON WEDNESDAY, AMBER finished her story just as the teacher told the kids to line up for recess.

"This looks terrific, Amber," I told her as it came out of the printer.

"Tomorrow you can do your drawings, okay?"

She nodded and I walked over to say goodbye to Dorito.

"Daddy," he said. "My zipper's stuck again."

"We have *got* to get you a new jacket," I told him as I tugged away. "This is ridiculous."

I finally got him zipped up and gave him a hug and a kiss goodbye.

"Can you come watch me at recess?" he begged.

"I don't know," I said, looking at my watch.

"Please?"

"I guess so," I finally agreed.

"Yea!" he said, scrambling to get in line.

At recess, I sat on the bench and watched him and Amber play. Just like he had told me, they played in the mulch under the slide, signing away with one another in some fantasy world they'd created.

But suddenly, as I was watching, I saw Amber cup her hands to Dorito's ear and then put her mouth up to them. Dorito left her and came running up to me.

"Hey, Daddy?"

"What?"

"Can Amber have this jacket when I get a new one?"

"Does she want it?"

"Uh-huh," he nodded.

"How do you know?"

"She asked me," he explained.

"How did she ask you?"

"She just *asked* me."

"Did she sign it?"

"No, she just asked. So can she have it?"

"Is that what she just did when she put her hands up to your ear?" I asked.

He nodded.

"But I thought you said she never talks!"

"She doesn't."

"Then how did she ASK you?"

"She whispered it," he said, as if I were an idiot. "Can she have my jacket?"

"She *whispers?*"

"Yeah. Can she-"

"YES! She can have your jacket if you get a new one," I said. "Dorito, *WHY didn't you tell me that she can whisper?*"

"Because," he said, shrugging. "You never asked."

Laci laughed when she heard Dorito's reasoning.

"He said that we always tell him not to talk in church – that he should whisper instead – so he figures they aren't the same thing."

"He's got a point," Laci agreed, as I pulled out my phone. "Who are you calling?"

"Danica."

"Interesting," Danica said after I'd filled her in on all the details.

"So what do you think?"

"It sounds like a classic case of select mutism, but obviously, without examining her myself, I can't be sure."

"So, let's assume you're right," I said. "What else can you tell me?"

"Select mutism used to be called 'elective mutism', but we don't use that name anymore because it suggests that the child is *choosing* not to talk, which is not the case. Like I told you, these are psychiatric

47

disorders and not just the result of the patient willfully choosing not to talk. If this is indeed what Amber has, she simply cannot talk in certain situations."

"What causes it?"

"Well, some research suggests that there's a biological deficiency going on, but I doubt that's what's solely to blame. Most anxiety disorders like this are the result of a combination of things."

"Like what?"

"Think about when Laci was depressed," Danica said. "She probably had an underlying biological condition that made her predisposed to depression, but she didn't actually *become* depressed until after Gabby died. It was a combination of things."

"So you think something bad like that's happened to her?"

"Well," Danica hedged, "I don't know. There's probably a reason for it, but the reasons aren't always clear. I mean, every little kid has had bad things happen to them. It's not necessarily some great trauma . . ."

"But it could be?"

"Sure."

"So, how does she get better?"

"Well, like I said before, she needs to be seeing a professional. I don't suppose you know yet whether or not she's being treated?"

"No."

"Because, I mean, there's definitely some stuff that can be done."

"Like drugs?"

"Well, sometimes anti-anxiety medications are used, but there's a lot of controversy about using them in children. I definitely think she needs to be receiving counseling. Sometimes a change in the environment can help. It really depends on the underlying causes."

"Is there anything I should know about working with her? Like, should I encourage her to talk to me, or is that just gonna make things worse?"

"I wouldn't push her too much," Danica said. "Offering her the option every now and then, however, isn't a bad idea — especially since select mutism tends to be self-reinforcing."

"What's that mean?"

"It means that people around the subject often stop expecting them to speak, and that can make it even more difficult for speech to occur."

"Okay, thanks," I said. "I got it."

"Need anything else?"

"Not right now."

"Well," she said, "I'll be glad to try and help any way I can. Feel free to call back anytime."

"Oh, don't worry," I said. "You know I will."

On Thursday, I worked with Christian and Mariah and then I stopped by Amber's desk and looked at her drawings.

"These look good," I said. "I like 'em."

She kept coloring.

"You know what?" I asked quietly, squatting down next to her desk.

She stopped coloring and looked at me.

"I saw you whispering to Dorito yesterday during recess."

She kept looking at me.

"You can whisper to me too," I said, and then I shrugged as if I didn't care. "You know . . . if you ever want to."

She didn't react.

"But you don't have to," I went on. "You can keep signing. Whatever. I just wanted to let you know that you can if you ever want to. Okay?"

Okay.

"Okay," I said. "I'll see you tomorrow. Bye."

Bye.

49

~ ~ ~

THE NEXT DAY was Friday and I was helping Drake. He was taking forever trying to decide what to say next in his new story and if he didn't hurry up I wasn't going to get to work with Amber at all today.

I found myself glancing over at her, and that's when I noticed Christian. He was leaning forward over his desk, talking to Amber. I couldn't hear what he was saying, but she had her head down and wouldn't look at him.

"Hang on for a second," I whispered to Drake, standing quietly and walking up behind Christian. He was hissing under his breath to Amber.

". . . ugly and everybody hates you and you stink like a skunk." He pinched his nose closed with two fingers and leaned even closer to Amber, trying to make sure that she would see him, even though her head was still down. "Pee-ew!"

I plopped down in between them on Amber's desk. Christian looked up at me in surprise.

"Hey, Amber," I said. "Go sit over there next to Drake, okay? I'm almost ready for you."

She rose from her desk without raising her eyes and walked obediently over to the computer area. I watched until she sat down and then I turned back to Christian, who was now suddenly very engrossed in coloring a page for his story.

"Hey, Christian!" I said quietly, leaning down into his face. "You think you're a big man? You little *fish killer?*"

He looked up at me worriedly and glanced across the room.

"Yeah, that's right. I know all about what you did to those fish. What'ya think Mrs. Spell would do if I told her about it?"

He gave me the slightest of shrugs.

"Think maybe she'd tell your parents?"

He looked as if he might cry.

"I wonder what *they* would do?"

50

I let him think about that for a minute and then I leaned down even closer into his face and whispered quietly.

"If I ever, EVER find out that you've talked to Amber like that again or that you've been mean to her, you're gonna have to deal with me," I said, jabbing myself in the chest with my thumb. "Do you understand?"

He nodded.

"Are you sure?"

He nodded again.

"Good," I said, smiling at him.

I walked back over to the computer, dragging an extra chair with me. I sat down between Drake and Amber.

"Okay, Drake," I said. "Did you figure out what you're gonna say next?"

"Maybe there's a whale following the boat and they start throwing cheese into the water for him? And then some seagulls land on his head and start eating the cheese?"

"Maybe," I agreed, "but it seems like you're kinda throwing something new in there and you're forgetting all about the pirates."

"Maybe the pirates could try to catch the seagulls?"

"But why? Why would the pirates do that when they're trying to find this island with a treasure?"

"I dunno," he shrugged.

"Look," I said. "How about this? You go back to your seat and draw a picture of the pirates finding the treasure. I want you to put everything in the picture that you want them to find – all the good stuff you can think of – and then tomorrow, when we meet, we can talk about exactly what you want to have happen on their way to the island, okay?"

"Okay," he said, getting up and heading off toward his desk.

"Hey, Amber," I smiled at her, patting Drake's empty seat. "Why don't you move over here?"

She moved over, but still kept her head down.

"How are you doing today?" I asked her.

She still didn't look up.

"What's the matter, Amber?"

No response.

"Amber," I said, leaning down and looking up into her face so that she had to see me. "Are you upset about something?"

She shrugged, refusing to make eye contact.

"About *that* guy?" I asked in disbelief, jabbing my thumb in Christian's direction.

She shrugged again.

"You've got to be kidding!" I said quietly. "You're gonna let something *Christian* says upset you?"

I leaned in closer to her.

"Amber, listen," I whispered conspiratorially. "You know what Christian is?"

For the first time she glanced at me.

"Christian's an idiot," I told her. "He's one half stupid and the other half dumb."

She kept her eyes on me.

"I heard what he was saying about you," I went on, "and he's absolutely wrong. He doesn't know what he's talking about. You're beautiful! You're the most beautiful little girl in this school! Don't you know that? You can't listen to somebody like Christian. He's an *idiot*."

She shifted slightly in her seat.

"You know what else?" I asked her. "You're the smartest, too!"

She looked at me uncertainly.

"Amber! You don't believe me?" I waved the folder with her story in it in front of her. "Look at what you've been doing! Do you see any other kid in here writing a story like you are?"

She lifted her head and looked at the folder.

"And you're doing it all on the computer – all by yourself!" I went on. "Nobody else is doing that. Nobody has an imagination like you do! Every day I come in here and I can't wait to see what you're going write next. I'll bet you're going to be a famous author one day."

She was still looking at me.

"Will you write some for me now?"

She shook her head and put her head down again.

"Please?"

She just shook her head some more.

"Okay," I sighed. "You don't have to write anything today, but will you please work on it with me on Monday?"

She nodded.

"Promise?" I asked.

She looked up and nodded again.

"Great," I said, smiling at her. "And don't forget what I said. You're the most beautiful girl in this whole school."

The next week was Thanksgiving week and the kids only had two days of school. I was shocked when I saw Amber on Monday. I told Laci all about it as soon as I got home.

"I think she was really upset about what Christian said to her and I think she went home and tried to make herself smell better."

"And did she?"

"I don't know," I said. "It was a *different* smell on top the other smell. She smelled like she'd sprayed herself down with air freshener or something."

"Poor thing."

"I think she tried to make herself look better, too," I said. "She cut her hair."

"She did?"

"I mean . . . I think she cut it by herself."

"Uh-oh," Laci said.

"Remember that big rat's nest I told you about?" Laci nodded and I went on. "I told you I didn't see how it was ever going to come out? Well, I think she *cut* it out."

"Does it look bad?" Laci asked, worriedly.

"It looks beyond bad," I said. "It looks horrible. There's this huge chunk missing in the back."

"Poor thing," Laci said again, shaking her head. "Do you think she could cover it up if she pulled it back into a ponytail?"

"Maybe," I said.

"I hope nobody teases her."

"If Christian teases her, I'm gonna pound his face into the ground."

"You know," Laci said, "it's not Christian's fault that he acts the way he does. He's probably learning his behavior from his parents, and he's probably very insecure and needs just as much attention and support as Amber does."

"Sorry," I said. "Somebody else is gonna have to take on Christian. I can only help one emotionally needy child at a time, and right now, Christian ain't it."

Tuesday morning I called Amber over to the computer first, even though it wasn't her turn.

"Look what I found!" I said, pulling out a picture. "You know who this is?"

Amber shook her head.

"This is J. K. Rowling," I told her. "You know . . . she's the one who wrote all the Harry Potter books you've been reading?"

Obviously interested, Amber looked at the picture more closely.

"You know who I think she looks like?"

Amber shook her head.

"I think she looks like you!"

She looked at me, questioningly.

"I do," I nodded. "Look at her. Her hair's the same color as yours and she's got such a pretty face. Don't you think you look like her?"

No.

"Well, of course she's a lot older than you in this picture, and her hair's back in a ponytail . . ."

54

(Apparently J. K. Rowling didn't wear ponytails very often, because it had taken me *forever* to find a picture of her with her hair in one.)

"You ever wear your hair in a ponytail?" I asked casually.

Shrug.

"I bet you'd look *just* like her with your hair in a ponytail."

She looked at me and blinked.

"Hey! You know what?" I asked her. "I might have one of my little girl's ponytail holders in my pocket. Let me see."

I fished around for the ponytail holder I'd stolen off of Lily's dresser that morning. "Yep! I do. You wanna try it and see if you look like J. K. Rowling?"

She blinked at me again and gave me a tiny nod.

"Here," I said. "Do you know how to put it in?"

She took it from me and proceeded to pull her hair back.

Much better.

"Wow!" I said. "I think you *really* look like J. K. Rowling! That looks great! You should wear your hair like that every day! I think it looks very pretty."

She blinked at me again.

"You wanna keep this?" I asked, holding the picture toward her. Amber nodded.

"You can keep the ponytail holder too, if you want."

Thank you, she signed.

"You're welcome," I said. "You know, you write such good stories, I really do think you're gonna be a famous author yourself one day! You might as well start looking like one."

I think I almost got a smile from her.

"You ready to get typing?"

Yes.

"Okay," I said. "Let's get going."

After Amber had typed for about fifteen minutes, I sent her back to her desk and told her to work on some of her illustrations. Then I called Mariah over and worked on a new story with her until Mrs. Spell told them to line up for recess.

I told my group to have a great Thanksgiving and everyone started scrambling around, putting their stories and drawings in their desks. I pulled on my jacket and then I said goodbye to Dorito. I was headed to the door when I felt a tug on my jacket. Amber had appeared at my side with a piece of paper. She held it up to me.

"What's this?" I asked, taking it from her. She pointed at me.

"This is for me?"

She nodded.

"Well, thank you!" I said, squatting down next to her. "Let's see what we've got here."

It was a picture of two people – a big person and a little person.

"Who is this?" I asked, pointing to the big person. She pointed at me.

"Me? Wow, that looks just like me. You did a good job. Look at that – his shoes are the same as mine and everything. Okay, who's this? Is this you?"

She nodded.

"Wow!" I said. "A picture of you and me. I love it! Thank you, Amber! I'm going to hang this on my refrigerator as soon as I get home so I can look at it every day!"

It was then that she rewarded me with my very first, small smile.

Then Amber bit her lip and pointed to the picture again, this time to the little person's hand.

"What?" I asked. "Is she holding something?"

Amber shook her head and I looked again.

"Umm–"

Amber held her own hand up in the "I Love You" sign.

"Oh!" I said, seeing it now. "She's saying 'I love you!'"

Amber nodded.

"Oh!" I said again. "That's fantastic. I like it even more now!"

She started to turn away.

"Hey, wait! Amber?"

She stepped back to me.

"I love you, too," I whispered, and then she darted off.

At lunch, I was handing Lily a slice of cheese out of the fridge when my phone rang. She attacked the cheese with a cookie cutter as I looked at the display on my phone. It was Scott.

"Vacation's over, buddy."

"What happened?"

"Apparently someone added Aqua-Naught," he said. Aqua-Naught was an additive used to make concrete dry faster than it would with just plain water. "I guess they didn't know that it had calcium chloride in it."

Calcium chloride was corrosive. Calcium chloride was *not* on the list of approved materials for construction with steel support beams and steel cables.

"So, whose idea was that?" I asked.

"You mean it wasn't yours?"

"Not funny, Scott."

"They're still investigating," he chuckled, "and I have no doubt we're gonna get sued along with everyone else who ever worked on it, but *we* know we're not responsible. Now get back to work."

"I'm kind of gonna need my computer," I said.

"They're keeping it . . . it's still evidence," Scott explained. "A whole new set-up should be there by Monday."

"So, technically my vacation's not quite over yet?"

"Enjoy your Thanksgiving, but come Monday you'd better start burning the midnight oil."

"Actually, I can't wait to get back to it," I said.

"Thanks for hanging in there, Dave," Scott said, seriously. "I know it hasn't been easy."

"No problem," I said, spying the picture from Amber on the fridge. "It hasn't been all bad."

~ ~ ~

"I'M GONNA KEEP on volunteering," I told Laci.

"But . . . I thought you said you were supposed to start back to work Monday!" she said.

"I am," I answered, "but I figure I can just work a little later in the evenings and not take so long for lunch and stuff."

"Okay," she said, hesitantly.

"What's the matter?" I asked "I thought you wanted me to volunteer."

"I did, but I–"

"It was your idea in the first place!" I reminded her.

"I know," she said, "and that's fine if you want to keep on doing it. I'm just surprised, that's all. I thought you'd quit once you started working again."

"I can't just walk away now when Amber's making so much progress!"

Laci smiled at me.

"You're totally smitten with her, aren't you?" she asked.

"No, I'm not," I said. "I just want to help her."

"Like you wanted to help Dorito when he had rickets?"

"I guess."

"And you weren't smitten with him?" she asked, still smiling.

I didn't say anything for a moment.

"She smiled at me today," I finally said.

"What?"

"I've never, ever seen her smile before," I explained. "But she smiled at me today."

"Oh, yeah," Laci said, nodding. "You're completely smitten."

It was our turn to have Thanksgiving dinner at our house. Laci's parent's came, my parents, my sister Jessica and her family, and of course, Charlotte and Mrs. White.

58

Jessica and her husband, Chris were talking all about their new house that they were building just outside of town and were showing us blueprints and pictures.

"We're gonna have a pond in the backyard," my nephew CJ told Dorito.

"With fish in it?" Dorito asked.

"Of course," Chris answered.

"I want a pond!" Dorito exclaimed.

"Yeah, right," Jessica laughed. "Like your daddy's ever gonna move out of this neighborhood."

"Why would I ever want to move out of this neighborhood?" I asked.

"So we can have a POND!" Dorito cried.

"Aw," I said, dismissing him with my hand. "Who needs a little ol' pond? We'll get ourselves a vacation house on Cross Lake instead."

"REALLY?" Dorito shouted

"Oh, brother," Laci said, looking at Chris. "Now see what you've done?"

"My lake's gonna be bigger than their pond," I said.

I was glad to see Amber when I got back to school on Monday. When I returned home, I found that all of my office equipment had arrived. By lunchtime, I had everything set up and was ready to go.

"Feel good?" Laci asked me, sticking her head in my office door after I'd been working for a couple of hours.

"Feels great!" I said, grinning at her.

"You still think you're gonna be able to tear yourself away every morning to go volunteer?"

"Pretty sure," I nodded.

The next morning, I was busy stapling Drake's story together while Christian and Mariah worked on their illustrations and Amber typed on the computer. I glanced over at her and she beckoned to me, so I set the stapler down and walked up to her. She motioned for me to come closer, so I leaned down and she cupped her hands to my ear.

"How do you spell clock?" she whispered.

She had never spoken to me before.

How do you spell clock?

I realized two things after I heard her say those words. First, I knew I would never forget the sound of her voice. Second, I realized that Laci had been absolutely right . . . I was completely smitten.

Mom called Wednesday evening.

"We need you to clean your stuff out of your room."

"What? Why?"

"Well," she said, "because we're going to have company, and they're going to be staying in your room."

"Why can't they stay in Jessica's room?"

"Because there's no bed in Jessica's room," she reminded me. They'd turned it into an office a few years earlier.

"Well, can't they just sleep in there the way it is, like Grandpa does?"

"Is there a reason you can't get your stuff out of here?" she asked. "I mean . . . you're almost twenty-nine years old. It's about time to leave the nest."

"I've left the nest!" I protested. "I just don't see why someone can't just stay there with it the way it is."

"Well, for one thing," she said, "they might be staying here for several weeks and I thought it would be nice if they could unpack and make themselves at home."

"Who is it?"

"No one you know."

"Well, who is it?"

"It's . . . it's someone who needs a place to stay for a while."

"Someone who needs a place to stay?"

"Yes."

"Why?"

"It's . . . it's complicated, David. We found out through someone at church that there's someone who needs a place to stay, and we offered to help out."

"Like a homeless person?"

"No, they're not homeless."

"Well, who is it?"

"It's no one you know," she said again.

"Well, tell me about them," I said. "Are they old? Young? Male? Female?"

"It's a young man," she said reluctantly.

"A young man?"

"Yes."

"How young?" I asked, envisioning a teenaged druggie hacking my parents to death while they slept.

"He's a little bit older than you."

"It's a grown man?" I asked. "Have you even met him?"

"Not yet."

"You're letting some strange man into your house?"

"Don't start overreacting."

"They could be a serial killer or something!"

"I'm glad you're not overreacting," Mom said.

"Okay," I admitted, "I might be overreacting a little bit, but is this a safe thing to do? I mean, do you really think it's a good idea?"

"I think it will be fine," she said.

"I don't think it's a good idea," I said.

"I didn't ask you what you thought," Mom said, and I could tell she was through trying to placate me. "I asked you if you'd come over here and get your stuff out of your room."

"Fine," I said. "When's he coming?"

"Not for a couple of weeks, but I'd like to do some cleaning and have time to get things ready, so I'd appreciate it if you could get your stuff out of here pretty quick."

"It would've been nice if you'd asked me to do this last week when I was still on suspension," I told her.

"Well, I'm sorry," she replied, not sounding sorry at all. "I didn't know about it then."

I was too busy catching up on all the work that I'd missed to put much thought into going over to Mom and Dad's. Saturday morning, Laci took the kids to run some errands and when they returned, Dorito told me that they'd seen Grandma at the library.

"She told me to tell you to get over there and get your stuff cleaned out of your room," Laci said.

"I know," I sighed. "I forgot."

"She said if you don't get over there pretty soon, she's not going to be responsible for what happens."

"What's that supposed to mean?" I asked.

"It means," she said, "that you need to stop clinging to your childhood and get over there and clean your stuff out of your bedroom. This guy's gonna be here in a couple of weeks!"

"I'm not clinging to my childhood!"

"Oh, please!" she cried. "Walking into your old bedroom is like entering a time warp! It's like a *shrine* in there! Everything's exactly the way it was before Greg died. All you gotta do is walk in there and suddenly you're seventeen again!"

"What's a shrine?" Dorito asked.

"I've been busy, Laci!"

"For ten years?"

"Yes! For ten years! I was at college for the first four years and then you dragged me down to Mexico–"

"And what have you been doing for the past two years?" she asked.

62

"Oh, I don't know," I said, waving my hand around the room. "Working maybe? Providing for my family?"

"What's a shrine?" Dorito asked again.

"Your daddy's old bedroom is a shrine," Laci told him with a smile.

"Fine," I said. "I'll call Scott and tell him I'm taking another week off so I can go clean up my room."

"It's going to take you a *week?*" she asked.

"Probably," I said. "And I'm probably going to get fired."

"What's fired mean?" Dorito wanted to know.

"It means we won't be able to live here anymore and *we'll* all have to move in to my old room at Grandma and Grandpa's," I explained sadly.

"Why don't you go over there and do it this afternoon?" she asked.

"It's my day off!" I protested.

"You just had four weeks off!"

"We're going to move in with Grandma and Grandpa?" Dorito asked happily.

"In your daddy's dreams," Laci laughed.

I set off to my parents' house and let myself in, dragging empty cardboard boxes behind me. Mom was out, but Dad was lying on the couch, watching football.

"Need some help?" he asked.

"No, thanks," I said. "I think I wanna do it myself."

He nodded, understanding.

I stopped in the doorway of my bedroom and looked around before I went in.

My schedule from my senior year in high school was still stapled to a faded bulletin board over my desk and my baseball hat from my junior year was hanging on the headboard of my bed. My soccer cleats and shin guards were in the corner near my closet and on my desk I could see some blueprints I'd once worked on in Advanced Drafting.

I walked over to my desk. On top of the blueprints were some ticket stubs to a concert that Laci and Greg and I had gone to together and some unused graph paper. I opened my top desk drawer. Inside was an old take-out menu from *Hunter's* and the magnifying glass that Greg had given me.

I sighed. Laci was right . . . my room was a shrine.

I sat down in the desk chair and opened the bottom drawer. Inside, I found the yearbook from our senior year in high school, still encased in shrink-wrap.

I tore the plastic off and opened it up, only having to turn a few pages before I found the dedication to Greg and his dad that I knew would be there. They'd given it more space than I'd imagined . . . apparently I wasn't the only one they'd had a big impact on.

The first two pages were a collage of pictures of them both. Some of them together; many of Greg with his friends. Not surprisingly, I was in a lot of them . . . so was Laci. I turned the page and found letters written to Greg by his classmates and turned it again to find ones written to Mr. White by his students. Of course, there was nothing on either page from me.

I'd been a mess that whole first year after they'd died and everything was pretty much a blur. I was sure, however, that if someone from the yearbook committee had dared to approach me to ask if I'd wanted to contribute something, I'd probably have walked away without answering.

But that was a long time ago. Now I looked at the pictures, and I read all the letters . . . it took me a long time. When I finally finished, I stood over my desk and scrounged around until I found a pen that worked and then I flopped back down on the floor next to the yearbook.

64

I found some space under a picture of Greg and his dad holding a rocket (I remembered we'd set it off later that day). I wrote:

I miss you both more than you'll ever know, but I'm sure you wouldn't have it any other way. I'll be seeing you relatively soon - love, Dave

And Laci thought I was clinging to my childhood.

~ ~ ~

LACI WAS DISMAYED when I came home empty-handed.

"What were you *doing* all that time?" she wailed.

"I'll have you know," I informed her, "that I'm pretty much done. I've got a few boxes left in my room that I have to bring back here, but I didn't have room for them in my car because it was so slam-packed full of stuff to go to the Salvation Army."

"And did you actually *go* to the Salvation Army?" she asked doubtfully, "or is everything still in your car?"

"No," I said proudly. "You'll be glad to know my childhood is totally gone . . . soon to be distributed amongst the less fortunate people of Cavendish. I am completely living in the present."

"Right," she laughed. "I'll believe that until you tackle someone on the street after you've spotted them wearing your swim championship t-shirt or something."

"That's in one of the boxes I'm keeping," I told her. "I'm not *insane.*"

On Monday, Dorito begged me to stay and watch him play at recess again after I'd finished volunteering.

"Okay," I said, "but just for a few minutes. I've got work to do."

I sat on the bench while Dorito and Amber watched their frosty breath come out of their mouths. The forecast was for snow and I could hardly wait to take Dorito and Lily sledding.

"She's come a long way since you've started working with her," I heard a voice say. I looked up and saw the teacher's assistant, Ms. Amy, standing near me.

"Oh," I said. "Thanks. I'm glad I can help."

She sat down next to me.

"We had no idea she could read and write," Ms. Amy said. "That was a good idea . . . using sign language."

66

"Dorito thought of it," I shrugged.

"Mrs. Spell told her foster parents about it," Ms. Amy went on, "in case they wanted to start taking some sign language classes or something to work with her at home."

"She's in foster care?"

"Oh," Ms. Amy said. "I guess I wasn't really supposed to say that."

"Don't worry about it," I said. "I won't tell anyone."

"Amber's in foster care!" I told Laci the second I got home.

"She is?"

"Yeah," I nodded. "I want to adopt her!"

"*Adopt her?*"

"Yeah!"

"You just met her a few weeks ago!" Laci protested.

"So? You wanted to adopt Lily, like, the first second after you saw her." Laci knew she had no argument for that.

"But I haven't even met her!" she said.

"Well, then come to school with me and meet her," I suggested.

"Well, I–"

"You'll love her, I promise!"

"Well, I'm sure I will, but–"

"I want to adopt her," I said again.

"What makes you think she's even up for adoption?"

"I don't see why she wouldn't be. I mean, foster care's for kids that don't have families . . . right?"

"I don't know," Laci said.

"Well, I'm gonna find out. I'm gonna call social services."

"You're serious?"

"Yes, I'm serious! Of course I'm serious. Why wouldn't I be serious?"

"Well . . . don't you think we should talk about it first?"

"What's there to talk about?" I asked, wrapping my arms around her. "I wanted Dorito, we got Dorito. Then you wanted Lily, we got Lily. Now it's my turn again and then you'll get to pick next."

She stared at me for a minute, curiously.

"If you meet her you'll be completely smitten, too," I smiled.

"You're crazy," she said, smiling back. That smile told me everything I needed to know.

"I'm calling social services," I said, squeezing her one more time and letting go. Then I went to find a phone book.

Right after lunch, we dropped Lily off with Laci's mom and soon found ourselves in the offices of the Department of Social Services – Child Welfare Division. We were assigned a caseworker, Brooke Williams, who met us in the reception area and then led us back to her tiny cubicle.

"Kind of cramped," she apologized, moving a stack of papers off of a chair so that we'd each have a place to sit down.

"No problem," I said.

"So, you are interested in adopting a foster child?"

"Yes," I nodded.

Brooke glanced at Laci, who nodded too and shot me a tiny smile.

"And you already have a specific child in mind?"

"Yes," I said. "Her name is Amber Patterson."

"Amber Patterson? That's not ringing a bell, let me see."

She started tapping away on her computer.

"She's in this state?"

"Yes," I said.

"I'm sorry," she said after a moment, "but we don't have any child by that name who's eligible for adoption."

"But she's in foster care," I said. "The teacher's assistant in my son's class told me so."

"Oh!" Brooke said. "I assumed you'd found her online through our website."

"No," I said.

"Well," she said. "Let me see what I can find."

She tapped away some more and then read her computer screen intently.

"I'm sorry," she said after a moment, turning away from the screen and looking at me. "Amber is not available for adoption."

"Why not?"

"I'm not allowed to discuss specifics about any of our cases," she said. "I'm sure you understand."

"But, if she's in foster care, then why can't we adopt her?" I persisted. "I mean, surely it would be better for her to be adopted into a permanent family than to just be in foster care, wouldn't it?"

"Let me just tell you about how our system works in general, without telling you anything specific about a particular case, okay?"

"Okay."

"Any time a family is unable to care for a child, or if the state determines that it's in the best interest of a child for them to be removed from their home, then the child becomes the responsibility of the state. These children are placed with certified foster care families whenever possible, or – if we don't have a placement available – into a group home.

"Now, you need to understand that our main goal is to return the child to their natural family whenever we can. Of course, sometimes that is not possible. For instance, if the parents are deceased and there were no other family members willing to take them in. Or if the child has been severely abused, it would be rare for the child to be placed back into the home. Usually, in a case like that, parental rights would be terminated by the state and the child then becomes adoptable. Often, the foster care family who has been caring for the child chooses to adopt the child. If not, they are placed on our state list of adoptable children.

"We have many, many children who are in foster care that are not adoptable. Remember, our main goal – whenever possible – is to return the child to their home. Unless parental rights have been terminated, foster children cannot be adopted."

"Can we become foster care parents?" I asked.

"We'd *love* to have you apply to be foster care providers, but not if you're only doing it because you hope to take Amber in. That's not going to be possible."

"Why not?"

"Children who are placed in the care of social services have usually been through a lot of trauma already. When we place a child, it's with the expectation that the child will remain with the same family until foster care services are no longer needed – either because they have been returned to their natural family or because they have aged out of the system. We avoid additional upheavals at all costs. We never move a child from one foster care family to another unless there's some kind of substantial justification for doing so."

"What kind of justification?"

"If the family requests that the child be removed, or if there's evidence that the child would be better off with another family."

"We still want to become a foster care family," I said, purposefully not looking in Laci's direction.

"Would you like to look through our list of adoptable children and see if maybe there's another child who–"

"No," I said. "But we want to become a foster care family."

"It's a rather lengthy process," she warned.

"That's okay."

"And you understand that even if you become certified, Amber won't be placed with your family?"

"Yes."

She looked at Laci.

"Are you both in agreement that you want to begin this process?"

I glanced at Laci, watched her nod, and breathed a silent sigh of relief.

"Okay, then," Brooke said, looking back to me. "Let's get started."

70

"What was *that* all about?" Laci cried as soon as we were outside.

"What d'ya mean?" I asked innocently.

"Why do you want to go through all this when you know we can't get Amber?" Laci asked, waving the thick packet of paperwork that Brooke had given us in front of her.

"She didn't say we couldn't get Amber," I said as we reached the car.

"Yes, she did! Honestly, David . . . what conversation were you a part of in there?"

"No," I corrected, holding the door open for her. "She said we couldn't get Amber unless there was justification to remove her from her current home."

Laci got in, and I closed her door and then jogged around to the other side.

"But there is no justification," Laci said after I climbed in.

"Not yet," I argued, as I started the car, "but there will be."

"What are you talking about?"

"I don't know what's going on in that house, but I'd bet my life that something's not right. Amber does *not* need to be there."

"David," Laci said, "don't you think that maybe you're overreacting just a little bit?"

"What do you mean?"

"I mean . . . I think you really like this little girl for some reason and I think that you'd like to have her live with us, and so maybe you're kind of imagining that she's worse off than she really is? You know, convincing yourself that she needs to be with us?"

"No," I said, shaking my head. "Something is *wrong*."

I glanced at Laci and she looked at me dubiously.

"Look," I said. "Why don't we have lunch with Dorito tomorrow in the cafeteria? Then you can meet Amber and see for yourself. If you think things are great, I'll drop it."

"No, you won't," she laughed.

71

"Okay," I shrugged, "you're probably right, but why don't you come and meet her anyway?"

"Okay," Laci agreed. "I'd love to."

~ ~ ~

DORITO WAS ECSTATIC that Laci and I were both going to
have lunch with him.

"Is Lily coming too?" he wanted to know.

"No," Laci explained, "Grandma's going to watch her so we can
spend some time with you."

And Amber.

Tuesday morning, I met with my group and told Amber that
Dorito's mommy was coming for lunch.

"Would you like to sit with us?" I asked, and she nodded.

I got home and started rifling through our filing cabinet, looking
for everybody's immunization records.

"Aren't you supposed to be working?" Laci asked.

"I just wanted to get started on finding some of this stuff that
DSS needs."

"I'll fill that stuff out," she said. "You get to work and earn some
money."

"When are you going to fill it out?" I wanted to know.

"Soon."

"When?"

"You promised I could meet her first and see what I think," she
reminded me.

I sighed, went into my office, and tried to concentrate on my
job. About thirty minutes before we needed to leave, I saved the file I
was working on and went downstairs to bug Laci.

"I wish you'd relax," Laci said after I'd paced around for a while.
She was sitting on the couch with Lily, reading a book to her.
"What's this, Lily? What's this?"

"Cow," Lily said.

"That's right. What's a cow say?"

"Mooooo."

"That's right. Good girl!"

"I can't relax," I said as Laci turned the page. "I can't wait for you to meet her!"

"Your daddy's silly," Laci whispered in Lily's ear, and Lily giggled.

Finally it was time to go. We loaded Lily up and dropped her off with Laci's mom again.

"Enjoy your lunch," she called as we were leaving.

"Obviously she hasn't had school cafeteria food in a while," I muttered as we closed the door.

After we arrived at the school, Laci and I checked in at the office, got our "Visitor" stickers, and headed down to the second grade hall. The kids were lining up as we arrived. Dorito and Amber were next to each other and I introduced Amber to Laci.

"Amber," I said, squatting down next to her, "this is Dorito's mommy. Her name is Laci."

"Hi, Amber," Laci said. "It's nice to meet you."

"Can you say 'Hi' to Laci?" I asked.

Amber took a loose strand of hair and put it in her mouth and looked at the floor.

"That's okay," I said, taking her hand. "Will you still eat with us?"

She looked at me and nodded.

"Good," I smiled, patting her on the back.

In the food line, we surveyed our options.

"Mmmm," Dorito said. "Tacos!"

"Mmmm," I agreed sarcastically, raising a knowing eyebrow at Laci.

"These are *not* tacos," Laci observed.

We weaved our way to the second grade table and sat down – Amber and Dorito directly across from me and Laci. I opened up one of my chocolate milks and smiled at Amber.

"Aren't we going to say grace?" Laci asked.

"Are we allowed to do that here?" I wondered.

Laci glared at me. "We're saying grace."

I peeked during grace and watched Amber. She didn't bow her head or close her eyes. She just eyed us curiously.

After we were finished, Amber leaned toward Dorito and pulled him to her. She cupped her hands around his ear and put her mouth to them.

"Oh," Dorito said after she sat back. "Because this isn't how they make tacos in Mexico."

Amber looked at Dorito questioningly and Dorito looked at Laci.

"My mom makes 'em like they do in Mexico," he explained. "She uses a . . . what do you use, Mommy?"

"Tortilla," Laci said.

"Yeah, tortilla," Dorito nodded. "And she doesn't use hamburger. What do you use, Mommy?"

"Well, you can use beef, but it isn't usually ground up like hamburger is. I usually use chicken, but a lot of people use pork."

Amber cupped her hand to Dorito's ear again and then Dorito asked, "What's pork?"

"Pig," Laci answered.

"Yeah," Dorito said. "Pig. And she puts the meat in this bowl with all this stuff that smells really good, and then she cooks it and puts it on the . . ."

He looked at Laci again.

"Tortilla," she smiled.

"Yeah. And then she chops up all this stuff and puts it on there, and then she puts this green stuff on there . . ."

"Guacamole."

"Yeah, guacamole. And then she makes this sauce to put on it. It's really good."

"You should come to our house sometime and Dorito's mommy could make you some," I suggested. "Would you like that?"

Amber nodded.

"You can come home one day with Dorito and have tacos with us. Okay?"

She nodded again.

"Her hair looks awful!" Laci exclaimed in a low voice as we left the school. I should have known that would be the first thing she zeroed in on.

"At least she's been keeping it in a ponytail," I said. "Trust me, it looks a whole lot better than it did."

"Why would her foster parents not take her to a beauty shop or something and get it fixed?" Laci asked.

"I don't know, Laci," I said. "Why would they let a giant rat's nest get in her hair in the first place? Why would they not make sure that she bathes or brushes her teeth? Did you *smell* her?"

"It was kind of hard to smell anything in that cafeteria."

"I bet she lives in a meth house," I said.

"Why do you think that?"

"Because I've heard about kids who live in meth houses smelling really bad like that."

"It could just be neglect."

"*Just* be neglect?"

"You know what I mean," she said.

"Meth, neglect, whatever. Don't you agree that she doesn't belong in that house?"

"Yeah," Laci nodded. "Something's wrong."

~ ~ ~

WEDNESDAY WE SET up an appointment for our first home inspection and after that we went down to the police station and had our fingerprints taken so that DSS could do a background check on us. Later I went to my dad's office (who also happened to be our accountant) and got all of our tax records, and that night we attended the first of seven classes required for families hoping to be certified.

One of the things they did in class that night was to show us a video dramatizing some of the things that kids might have gone through before they became a ward of the state. Both Laci and I were pretty quiet on the way home.

"I . . . I hate that she went through something like that," Laci finally said.

"I hate to think that she's going through something like that right now!" I said. "We've got to get her out of there."

"I don't understand how you're going to convince DSS that she needs to be out of that house."

"I'm going to find some kind of evidence to show them that they're not taking good care of her!"

"How?"

"I'm not sure," I admitted, "but we need to get the rest of that paperwork filled out because after I get her out of there, she's coming home to live with us."

I truly didn't know what to do to obtain the evidence that I needed, but I started by offering to pick up Dorito after school on Thursday. I got there early . . . very, *very* early. The procedure at the elementary school was to load up all the kids who rode the bus first and then to start calling kids out who were car riders. I was third in line and had a front row seat to watch the kids as they boarded the bus.

77

I had taken note of what Amber was wearing that morning and I easily recognized her as she came out of the building and trudged up the steps of her bus.

Bus 884.

Friday afternoon I let Laci and Lily pick Dorito up after school. Laci didn't know it, but I was at the school too – parked in the parking lot, with my motor running.

When Bus 884 pulled away, I left my parking spot and followed it into town. Trailing a bus (it turns out) is very, very easy.

The bus had been dropping kids off for about half of an hour when I finally saw Amber get off all by herself. We were in an older neighborhood with large lots, ancient maple trees and a vast assortment of homes. I pulled over alongside the curb and watched as she walked up to a split-level house with overgrown shrubs. She reached into the front pocket of her book bag and pulled out a key. Then she opened the door, let herself in, and closed the door behind her.

"She's only in the second grade!" I cried to Laci when I got home. "I can't believe she's going home to an empty house and having to let herself in!"

"I can't believe you were following her!" Laci said. "Isn't stalking illegal in this state?"

"I wasn't *stalking* her!" I insisted. "I'm just trying to figure out what's wrong and I've already found out one thing . . . there's nobody there to take care of her when she gets home! *That's* what's illegal! Isn't that illegal?"

"I . . . I don't know, David."

"Well, it *should* be illegal!" I said. "I mean, we're filling out all this paperwork to become a foster care family and they're worried about

78

whether we have carbon monoxide detectors in our house or if we've ever had a *speeding* ticket, but they're okay with a second grader coming home to an empty house every day?"

"You don't know that it's every day."

"I bet DSS doesn't know about this," I said.

"Are you going to tell them?"

"Of course I am!"

"Do you really think this would be grounds for getting her removed?"

"Maybe not," I said. "But I bet there's a lot more going on than just this."

I called DSS and told them I needed to speak with Amber Patterson's caseworker.

"Let's see," the receptionist said. "That would be Erin Lamont. Let me see if she's available."

"Erin Lamont," a voice answered after the third ring.

"Um, hello," I said. "My name is David Holland."

"Yes, Mr. Holland," she said. "What can I do for you?"

"Well, um, I'm calling about Amber Patterson. I'm . . . I'm really concerned about her welfare."

"Why is that?"

"Well, um, I think she's being neglected."

"Why do you suspect that?"

"It doesn't seem that anyone is really taking care of her properly. I mean . . . I don't think she's getting bathed regularly and she cut this big chunk out of her hair that looks really bad and I don't think she's brushing her teeth . . ."

"I see," she said. "What was your name again?"

"David Holland."

"Okay. And how do you know Amber?"

"I do some volunteer work at Bluefield Elementary. She's in the same class with my little boy. They're good friends."

"I see," she said again. "Okay, well, I appreciate the information and I'll certainly look into—"

"Wait!" I said. "She's also going home alone every day. I mean . . . she's only a second grader and she's going home alone to an empty house."

"And how do you know this?"

Isn't stalking illegal in this state?

"I, um, my son told me."

"I see. Okay, well, thank you for the information."

"So you're going to look into it?"

"Absolutely," she said. "Thank you."

"Okay," I said. "Thank you."

~ ~ ~

MONDAY MORNING, AMBER started on a new story about
an elephant who escaped from the circus and found a job in a peanut
factory. That afternoon – after I'd given her social worker plenty of
time to investigate what I'd told her – I drove down to DSS.

When I walked into the lobby, the receptionist looked up at me.

"David Holland, right?" she asked. Laci and I had been in there
quite a bit last week, dropping off various forms and documents.

"Right," I said.

"And you're here to see Ms. Williams?"

"Actually," I said. "I need to see Erin Lamont."

"Oh," she said. "I'm sorry. I could've sworn–"

"Brooke is our caseworker," I said. "But I need to see Ms.
Lamont about something else."

"Oh," she said. "Certainly. Let me tell her that you're here."

A few minutes later a woman came out and walked across the
lobby to me.

"Mr. Holland?"

"Yes. Hi," I said, standing up and shaking her hand.

"What can I do for you?" she asked.

"I just needed to talk to you for a minute."

"Do you need to come back to my office?"

"Yes, please," I said. "Thank you."

She led me down the hall, a few doors past Brooke Williams'
office. Unlike Brooke's office, Erin Lamont's office was neat and
tidy.

"Have a seat," she offered.

"Thank you."

"Now," she said after I'd sat down. "What can I do for you
today?"

"I was just wondering what you found out about Amber."

"I'm sorry, Mr. Holland. I'm not allowed to discuss that with
you."

"Oh."

"I'm sure you understand."

"But you, like, went out there and investigated, right?"

"I can't get into specifics."

"But, I mean, you can tell me that you followed up on what I told you, right?" I asked. "Even if you don't tell me what you found out?"

"Amber is fine."

"So, you looked into it?"

She didn't answer me for a moment.

"Mr. Holland," she finally said, taking a pencil from a cup on her desk and rolling it between her hands. "Why do you have such an interest in this child?"

"I'm just worried about her," I said.

"No other reason?"

"No."

"Are you sure?"

"Yes," I said. "I'm sure. Why?"

"Because, actually," she said, tapping the pencil on her desk. "I looked into you."

"What?"

"Just a quick search . . . to see if anything popped up."

I didn't say anything.

"I was surprised," she went on, "to find that you and your wife have recently applied to be foster parents."

"Yes," I answered.

"I believe your caseworker is Brooke Williams?" she asked, pointing her thumb down the hall.

"Yes."

"I had a conversation with her," Erin Lamont nodded slowly, putting the pencil to her lips. "From what I understand, you initially came in because you were hoping to adopt Amber?"

"Um, well, yes."

"But then – when you found out she wasn't eligible for adoption – you suddenly decided you were interested in becoming foster parents."

"Yes."

"I couldn't help but wonder if perhaps you were going through the certification process for the sole purpose of getting Amber?"

"Well," I said, shifting uncomfortably in my seat, "I mean, if she became available, obviously we'd be interested, but that's not why we're getting certified."

She eyed me.

"Ms. Williams explained to you that Amber wouldn't be moved out of her current home unless there was justification."

"Right."

"I'm wondering," she said, tapping the pencil again, "if maybe you're looking for reasons why Amber shouldn't be in her current home because you want her in *your* home."

"No!" I said. "I . . . I'm just worried about her. I had a concern and I called you about it. I thought that's what you're supposed to do!"

"No ulterior motive?"

"No!" I said, shaking my head.

"I hope not," she said, putting the pencil back into the cup. "Our office has to put in many, *many* hours for each and every family that goes through the certification process. It would be unethical of you to try to get certified in the hopes of getting a child you've been told is not available."

"I'm not," I said, weakly.

"Wonderful," she said, standing up. "Is there anything else I can do for you?"

"No."

"Wonderful," she said again, reaching out to shake my hand. "Have a great evening."

~ ~ ~

TANNER AND I had reserved a racquetball court for seven o'clock that evening. Before we got out of the locker room, I'd told him everything.

"Do you think she even looked into what you told her?" Tanner asked.

"No. I think as soon as she figured out what I was up to she just blew the whole thing off."

"So what are you gonna do?"

"I'm gonna stake out that house until I get some evidence she can't ignore."

"Are you serious?" Tanner asked.

"Yeah."

"I wanna go on a stake out!" he exclaimed.

"You've always secretly wanted to be a spy, haven't you?" I asked, and he grinned at me.

"Seriously, though," he said as we left the locker room. "I wanna help."

"Really?"

"Heck, yeah!" he said, except that he didn't really say "heck."

"I can use all the help I can get," I admitted.

"Is it legal?" he asked.

"Do you care?"

"No, not really," he admitted. "I just wondered."

"I have no idea," I said. "Laci seems to think not."

"She's probably right," he agreed.

"Wanna start tonight?"

"Oorah!" Tanner grunted.

"Oorah?"

"Haven't you ever seen *Jarheads* with Jamie Fox?"

"I'm afraid not," I said as we reached our court.

"It's a classic," Tanner said, opening the door. "You should see it. But anyway . . . you know! *Oorah* is what they say in the military when they're ready to go do something!"

"You're not in the military," I pointed out.

"I know," he said. "But I'm not really a spy, either."

We only played two games instead of our usual three or four (he slaughtered me in both games, just in case you're wondering) and then we cleaned up. We left my car in the parking lot at the YMCA and hopped into his truck.

When we got to Amber's house we parked across the street and one door down.

"Now what?" Tanner asked.

"How do I know?" I said. "You're the one who's always wanted to be a spy."

"We need a camera," Tanner mused.

"For what?"

"Evidence."

"What kind of evidence?"

"I dunno," he shrugged. "You said you needed evidence. Seems to me you need a camera if you need evidence."

"Okay," I said. "I'll bring ours next time."

"We need some doughnuts, too."

"We could go knock on the door and ask them if they've got any," I suggested.

"Who keeps doughnuts around the house?"

"We've got doughnuts," I said.

"You do?"

"Yeah. Those little mini, powdered sugar ones."

"Why didn't you bring 'em?" Tanner asked.

"Trust me," I answered. "If I'd known I was bringing you along, I would have. I promise I'll be better prepared next time."

"You'd better be."

We sat there for about an hour, but saw absolutely no activity.

"I'm gonna go see if I can see in the basement windows," Tanner said.

"Seriously?"

"Sure," he said. "Why not?"

"Ummm . . . 'cause you might get arrested?"

"You're a lousy spy," Tanner said.

"I know," I replied. "That's why I brought you along."

"I'll be back in a minute," he said.

It was more like *fifteen* minutes. My stomach was in knots the whole time he was gone.

I was staring intently at the house, imagining what I was going to tell Laci if one or both of us got arrested, when suddenly there was a loud rap on my window.

I spun around to find Tanner's face pressed against the glass. He laughed at me and then jogged around the front of the truck and climbed in.

"What are you scaring me like that for?" I yelled after he closed his door.

"I wanted to see if I could make you jump," he said.

"Congratulations."

"Do you need to change your pants?" he asked.

"Just about."

"You never even saw me, did you?"

"No."

"I'd make *such* a good spy."

"So, what'd ya find out?!"

"Well," he said, "the basement windows are all blocked. You can't see anything through any of them."

"Blocked?"

"Yeah, thick black curtains on some of 'em. Cardboard with duct tape on other ones."

"Why?" I said.

"Obviously they don't want anybody seeing what's going on in there."

86

"Really?"

"Oh, yeah," he said, nodding. "I mean, I can see wanting your privacy and putting some curtains up or whatever, but this is different. There's no way to see *anything* in any of those lower windows. Who's that careful unless they're hiding something?"

"Do you think they're running a meth lab?" I asked him.

"What makes you ask that?"

"Remember how I told you she smells really bad? I've heard about kids who are living in meth houses smelling really bad."

"Could be," Tanner said. "Something's going on in there, that's for sure."

"What should I do?"

"Let me think on it for a while," Tanner suggested. "We'll figure out a way to find out what's going on."

"You really would make a good spy."

"I'd also make a very good serial killer."

"Trying to scare me again?" I asked.

"No," he said, matter of factly. "I'm just saying. I think I'd be a really good serial killer."

"Good to know."

"They'd never be able to catch me," he mused.

"Great," I said.

"You wanna sit here any longer?"

"With a serial killer?"

"I mean, I don't mind staying longer if you want to," he said.

"No, I guess not. I don't see the point," I said. "It's not like they're gonna come out onto the lawn and start baking meth or something."

"*Baking meth?*"

"Yeah."

"I think it's called *cooking* meth."

"Whatever. You wanna go?"

"Yeah," he agreed. "Probably there's not gonna be much *meth baking* going on tonight."

~ ~ ~

BY THE END of the week Amber had finished her story about the elephant. After he had escaped from the circus, he'd obtained a job working in a peanut factory, but was quickly fired because he kept eating the profits. After a brief stint at a cheese factory (which didn't work out because there were too many mice), the elephant had found happiness working at a car wash. I personally thought it was a particularly brilliant story.

On Saturday – three days before Laci was scheduled to fly to Texas – my mom called.

"You need to get over here and get the rest of your stuff out of your room," she told me.

"What stuff?"

"All those boxes in the closet."

"How are they hurting anything in the closet?" I asked.

"I can take them to the dump for you if you'd like," she said.

"I'll get them," I sighed.

"Today?"

"Well, I'm supposed to play racquetball with Tanner this afternoon," I said.

"Tomorrow?"

"Yeah," I said. "I'll get them tomorrow. Or Monday."

Now it was Mom's turn to sigh.

"I promise," I said. "I'll get 'em by Monday."

"You'd better," she said. "Or they're going to the dump."

Tanner picked me up at my house on Monday during our regular racquetball time.

"You got doughnuts?" he asked.

"Yep," I said. "Brought the camera too."

"Your regular camera?"

"Yeah."

"Here," he said, handing me a bag. "Check this out."

I reached into the bag, pulled out a camera, and whistled.

Periodically my company sent me to areas that had experienced earthquakes. Part of my job was to inspect structures that had been minimally damaged and to assess whether or not they needed to be condemned. The company always provided us with good cameras to document our findings . . . but I'd never held one as nice as this.

"Whoa!" I said. "Where'd ya get this?"

"I bought it."

"When?"

"Today."

"Are you serious?" I asked.

"Yeah," he said. "You need to figure out how to work it. I don't have a clue. They put the lens on for me at the store."

"How much did it cost?"

"Nothing a month's worth of teaching unruly teenagers won't cover."

"I hate that you spent a bunch of money on this," I said. "I'll be glad to pay you for it."

"I don't need your money," he answered, sounding offended.

"No, I didn't mean that, but—"

"Just shut-up," he said, cutting me off, "and figure out how it works."

I turned the dome light on and played with it until we got to Amber's street. Then I turned the light off as Tanner pulled up to the same spot we'd parked in the week before.

"Got it figured out?" he asked.

"I think so," I said.

I held the camera up to my eye and focused on a mailbox that was about fifty yards away. I snapped a picture and then viewed it on the screen.

"The resolution on this thing is unbelievable," I said as I zoomed in on it. "This lens is amazing."

"It better be," Tanner said. "It cost twice as much as the camera."

I wanted to offer to pay him for it again, but I kept my mouth shut.

"So you're gonna be stuck home with the kids for the rest of the week?" Tanner asked.

"Yep. Laci leaves tomorrow morning."

"She excited?"

"Yeah," I sighed.

"Aren't you happy for her?" he asked.

"For what?"

"That she's getting to do something she really loves."

"You don't think she loves being a stay-at-home mom?"

"No," he said. "I don't mean that. I just mean that she got her degree specifically so she could go to work *for that organization*, and I just . . . I just can't help but wonder if she doesn't miss it."

"She misses it," I admitted. "I know she does."

"Well you can work from anywhere," he said. "So why are you here?"

"You trying to get rid of us?"

"No," he said. "You know I love having you guys home, but I guess I've never really understood *why* you're home."

"Laci felt like God told her to come home," I explained. "I wasn't about to argue with either one of them."

"What if He tells her to go back?"

"That's what I'm afraid of."

"But would you go back?"

"Yes," I sighed.

"Really? Just like that? Laci says, '*Oh, I think God wants us to go back to Mexico!*' and you're just gonna take her word for it and go?"

"Yeah."

"But what if God tells you something different? What if He tells *her* one thing and *you* another thing?"

"First of all, I don't think He'd do that," I said.

"What if He did?"

90

"Then . . . then I'd probably do what He was telling Laci."

"Why?"

"Because Laci's never been wrong about anything like that before," I said. "She's always seemed to have this direct pipeline to God and she's always done what He's told her to do and it's always turned out to be the right thing. My track record's not that great."

Tanner didn't ask any more questions and we were sitting quietly when a car came down the street and slowed to a stop in front of Amber's house. A teenage boy, smoking a cigarette, climbed out of the passenger seat and stood with the door open, talking to the driver for a moment. I snapped a few pictures for good measure.

"Hey!" Tanner said excitedly as the boy closed the door and the car drove off. "I know him!"

"Which one?"

"The one that just got out of the car!" he said, pointing as the kid flicked his cigarette into the yard and walked up to Amber's house.

"Who is he?"

"I don't know."

"I thought you said you knew him."

"Well," he explained, "I know him from somewhere. I just can't remember where."

"Well, think!" I insisted. "Did you coach him?"

"No," Tanner said, definitively.

The guy walked around the side of the house and disappeared into the back-yard.

"Did you teach him?"

"Maybe . . ." he said. "I can't remember."

"I wish I knew his name."

"What's Amber's last name?" he asked.

"Patterson."

"That's not ringing a bell," he said.

"But she's in foster care, remember? That won't be their last name."

"What's their last name?"

91

"I have no idea."

Tanner reached for his phone.

"What are you doing?" I asked.

"I'm gonna find out their last name."

"How?"

"I'm gonna call Sierra," he said.

"Who's Sierra?"

"Someone I used to go out with," he explained, scrolling through his contacts on his phone. "She sells real estate."

"How's she gonna help?"

"I think I can give her the address, and she can tell us whose name is on the deed."

"What if they're renting?" I asked.

"Then we won't know their last name, will we?"

He hit send and waited for a minute.

"Hey, Sierra! You got a second?"

"Anything for you, Tanner," I heard her say. I rolled my eyes at him.

"I've got an address that I was hoping you could tell me who owns it."

"You looking for a place?"

"No, but if I am you'll be getting the commission. Don't worry."

She laughed and asked him for the address.

"Seven thirty-nine South Drye Street."

She said something that I couldn't hear and he closed his phone.

"What'd she say?"

"She's gotta get to her computer and she'll call me back."

"Are you sure this is legal?"

"You're suddenly worried about legal?" Tanner asked.

"No. Just wondering."

"It's legal," he said. "You and I could go down to the courthouse and find out if we wanted to, but it's easier for her. She's got some program on her computer."

"I don't understand how you know all this."

"I have my ways."

I shook my head.

"What?" he asked.

"What I really don't understand is how you love all these women and leave 'em and they still wanna talk to you afterward."

"It's a talent," he said.

"You ever talk to Megan?" I asked. Megan was the girl he'd lived with and then refused to marry when she'd claimed to be pregnant.

"Nope," he said. "I'm not that talented."

I shook my head again.

We waited about ten minutes before Sierra called him back.

"Hey, Babe," he said. "What ya got?"

He scribbled something down, promised to get together with her sometime, and closed his phone again.

"Wayne and Rebecca Trent," he said.

"Does that name ring a bell?" I asked.

"I . . . I don't know," he said. "Maybe."

"You're a big help."

"Sorry," he said.

~ ~ ~

TANNER CALLED ME at three o'clock in the morning.

"Hello?"

"I remembered who he is," Tanner said.

"Really?"

"Yeah. How 'bout I pick you up in about ten minutes and we go to the high school so I can get some copies made?"

"Copies of what?"

"Just some handouts for class next week."

"You're gonna go to the school in the middle of the night to make copies?"

There was a very long pause.

"You're really dense," he finally said, "you know that?"

"Oh."

"So are you gonna be ready in ten minutes or not?"

"I'll be ready," I said. "Oorah."

"*Oorah?*" Laci asked, lifting her head and looking at me as I turned on the light.

"It's a military term," I informed her, climbing out of bed. "You wouldn't understand."

"What are you doing?" she asked as I pulled on a pair of jeans.

"Tanner and I are gonna go do something."

"*Now?*"

"Apparently."

"What are you going to do?"

"I'm not exactly sure."

"Is it going to be something *legal?*"

"I'm not exactly sure."

"You're both going to get arrested," she said, putting her head back on the pillow.

"Maybe," I admitted.

"If you need someone to bail you out, do me a favor and call your dad, okay? I've got a plane to catch tomorrow."

94

"Okay," I said. "No problem."

"Anthony," Tanner said when I climbed into his truck. "His name's Anthony Perry."

"Did you teach him?"

"Sort of," Tanner replied.

"Sort of?"

"Two years ago I had a split position. I had two physical education classes and the other half of the day I worked ISS."

"In-School Suspension."

"Yeah."

"And let me guess. This Anthony kid was in there?"

"All the time," Tanner nodded. "He spent more time in in-school suspension and out-of-school suspension than he did in regular classes. Toward the end of the year, though, he quit showing up. I think he dropped out."

"What grade was he in?"

"I think he was a freshman," Tanner said, "but I'm not sure. We're gonna take a look at his records when we get to the high school and see what we can find out."

"What kind of records? Like his grades?"

"I think we'll find some other stuff too."

"Like what?"

"Well, once I remembered who he was, I got thinking about it. When kids get sent to ISS, all their regular school work gets sent down there for them to do – you know, whatever they were supposed to do in regular class they'd have to do in there with me, right?"

"Right."

"Even if they had to take a test or something."

"Uh-huh."

"So I remember that whenever he had to take a test, his was always a read-aloud."

95

"A what?" I asked.

"A read-aloud."

"He had to read it out loud?"

"No," Tanner explained. "I always had to read the test out loud to him."

"Why?"

"Cause that's what was in his IEP."

"His what?" I asked.

"His Individualized Educational Plan. He was a special ed kid."

"Like . . . he was mentally retarded or something?"

"No, kids can get IEPs and 504s for all sorts of things. Learning disabilities, ADHD, autism . . . whatever. I bet Amber's got one."

"What's a 504?"

"I don't know exactly," Tanner said. "All I know is that kids with IEPs and 504s have files in the special ed office, and they have all sorts of information in them . . . like if you have to read the test aloud to the kid or if they get to be tested in a separate room or whatever they need."

"And you have access to his file?"

"Well . . ." he hesitated as we pulled up into the parking lot of the school.

"Laci's right," I muttered. "We're going to get arrested."

Tanner turned off the engine.

"I can look at the files of any student I'm teaching."

"But you're not teaching him now?"

"No."

"But you can get hold of his file?"

"I think so."

I bit my lip and looked through the windshield at the darkened school.

"What d'ya think?" Tanner asked after a minute.

This is illegal.

"Oorah?" he asked.

"Yeah," I finally nodded, reaching for the door handle. "Let's do it."

96

The first thing we did when we got to the high school was to go into the main office and turn on the central photocopy machine.

"What are we doing?" I asked as we waited for it to warm up.

"Making copies," Tanner said, opening a ream of paper.

I watched him take the top piece of paper from the stack and make several small tears in it. He opened the lid of the copier and then opened up a textbook. He laid the textbook face down on the glass as the copier beeped to let us know that it was ready. Next, he opened up the paper tray and placed the ream into it with the torn paper on top.

"Isn't that gonna jam the machine?" I asked. He rolled his eyes at me and hit "Start."

The machine whirred to life and we could hear it attempting to make a copy. Sure enough, it quickly beeped at us to let us know that there was a jam.

"Aw," Tanner said. "That's a shame. I hate it when that happens."

"We can probably fix it," I suggested.

"I don't think so," Tanner said. "I think we'd better go in there." He pointed to a door down the hallway.

"What's that?" I asked.

"EC Services," he explained.

"EC?"

"Politically correct way of saying special ed," he explained. "They've got a photocopy machine we can use since this one's jammed."

"Ohhhh," I said. "I get it."

"You finally got it figured out, Sherlock?"

We headed down the hallway and Tanner produced another key.

"You have a key to EC Services?"

"I have a master key."

"Do all the teachers have master keys?"

"Not exactly."

We entered the EC Services suite and Tanner flipped on a light. He headed toward a wall that was lined with filing cabinets. A photocopy machine was next to the filing cabinets and Tanner hit the "Power" button. Then, he started reading the labels on the drawers of the filing cabinets.

"This is the one, I think," he said, tapping one of them.

"Is it unlocked?"

He tried a drawer. "Of course not. That would be too easy."

"Are you gonna pick it?"

"I will if I have to," he said, "but I've got the keys to about seven filing cabinets on my key ring, and I'd bet almost anything that one of them will work."

"Why?"

"Because they're cheap filing cabinets, that's why."

"Shouldn't records like this be a little more secure than that?" I asked.

"Should be," Tanner agreed, trying the first key. "But that doesn't mean they are."

"You're a great spy," I told him as the lock popped open with the fourth key he tried.

"Thanks," Tanner grinned, opening the textbook he'd had in the main office and pointing to a page with nutritional information charts on it. "Here. Make thirty-two copies of this."

"Why?" I asked as he opened a filing cabinet drawer.

"Because I need it for class tomorrow, so you might as well make yourself useful. Besides, that's why we're in here, *remember?*"

"Oh, right," I said, taking the book from him.

He started looking through files as I made a single copy of the page.

"Do you really think anybody's gonna come in here?" I asked, pulling the copy out of the machine and assessing it.

"No," he said, closing the top drawer and opening up the next one down. "But I feel safer having an excuse for being in here."

"Me too," I agreed, grabbing a pair of scissors from a nearby work table.

"What are you doing?" he asked.

"What d'ya mean?"

"I mean, why are you *cutting?*"

"Because there's all this extra stuff that got copied," I said, holding the paper up to show him, "and I'm trimming it off before I run the final copies so it'll look nice."

"Oh, brother," Tanner said. "Just make the copies!"

"I can't make 'em look nice?"

"You do whatever you want," he sighed, shaking his head, "but you'd never make it as a teacher."

"I'd be an excellent teacher!" I insisted.

"Oh, please!" Tanner said. "I can just see their eyes glazing over while you bound around up in the front of the room talking about the joys of parabolas or something."

"Well," I said, "at least they'd be able to read the handouts I gave them!"

"Yes," Tanner said, turning back to the filing cabinet. "And that's what's *really* important."

I ran another copy and scrutinized it. It was covered with little black spots.

"You got any Wite-Out?" I asked Tanner.

"Here it is!" he said, pulling a file from the drawer.

"Really?"

"Yup!"

"What's it say?"

"Give me a second . . . you got those copies made?"

"Almost," I said, forgetting about the black spots. I hit "32" and then "Enter."

The copy machine spit out page after page as Tanner and I scanned through Anthony's file.

"Okay," Tanner muttered, flipping pages. "Specific learning disability in reading. That explains the read-aloud. This page just shows what kind of modifications we have to make to accommodate his special needs, and this one just shows that his parents agree to those modifications . . ."

"Wait!" I said. "Who signed that one?"

"Ummm . . . it's kind of hard to read," Tanner said. "Betty Trout, maybe?"

"Becky Trent?"

"Yeah. I think that's it."

"That's Rebecca Trent . . . her name was on the deed for the house, remember?"

"Good work, Sherlock," Tanner said. "You're not such a bad spy yourself."

"So we've got Anthony Perry and Amber Patterson living with the Trents. He must be a foster kid too."

"Probably," Tanner agreed. "Or a step-kid."

"If he's a foster kid, when's he gonna age out?"

"Ummm, looks like he just turned seventeen, so not for a while."

I sighed.

Tanner continued to flip through the folder as the photocopy machine came to a stop. I stepped away from the file for a second, taking out the original and the copies. Tanner stepped in right after me, loading several pages into the automatic feed slot and hitting the start button.

"What's that?"

"Ummm," he hesitated, "just something I wanna take a closer look at when we get outta here."

He grabbed the originals as they shot out of the automatic feeder and stuffed them back into the folder. I started to reach for the copies, but he grabbed them before I could.

"Let's go," he said, stuffing the folder back into the drawer. He pushed it shut and depressed the lock. "You got my copies for tomorrow?"

"Right here," I said, holding them up. He took them from me and put the copies he'd just made in the middle of my stack. Flipping off the lights as we went, Tanner closed the door to EC Services and

100

led us back through the main lobby and then out the front door of the building.

"So let me see what you copied," I said after we'd climbed back into the truck.

"Ummm, I think I'd better look at 'em first," he said, tucking them into a pocket in his door.

"Why?"

"I'm not even supposed to *tell* you anything about a student that I've taught, much less let you look at their files."

"But you already let me look at his file," I argued as he started the engine. "Why can't you just let me see what it is?"

"I just . . . I just think I'd better look at it first and then . . . then if there's anything you need to know, I promise I'll tell you."

"Why can't you show me now?" I persisted.

"Look, David," he said, turning toward me. "Will you trust me? I mean, I just broke the law for you. I could go to jail, get fired, lose my license. Will you just trust me? If there's something in here you need to know about, I'll tell you. Okay?"

"Okay," I said as he started the truck. But on the way back to my house, I thought about what he'd said.

I just broke the law for you. I could go to jail, get fired, lose my license.

What had gotten into me lately? Since when did I break the law? Since when did I jeopardize my best friend's job? Since when did I think it was okay to lie to a social worker . . . to tell her that I wanted to take in foster kids, when, really, I was only interested in getting the one child she'd already told us we couldn't have?

I knew the answer . . . it had been since I'd met Amber. Since I'd decided that she was in trouble and that she needed me.

But that's okay, right? Wasn't bending the rules acceptable if you were trying to help someone? Didn't we lie to Charlotte to keep her and Jordan from finding out about Chase? Didn't mission workers sneak the Gospel into countries where it was illegal all the time? Wasn't this pretty much the same thing?

Part of me knew that I needed to talk to God about it – that I needed to find out what He thought. Part of me knew that I should pray about it and listen to God and make sure that I knew His will.

But another part of me was afraid to find out God's will. I desperately wanted Amber, and I wanted to get her out of that house, and I really didn't want to hear about it if God didn't feel the same way.

That part of me was the bigger part.

And so – on the ride home in Tanner's truck – I convinced myself that what I was doing was right and that God must surely be okay with it.

After all, how could God possibly want anything else for that sweet little girl, except for what I already knew was right?

~ ~ ~

THE NEXT MORNING I took Dorito to school and volunteered for the last time until after the holidays.

"I'm not gonna see you until after break," I told Amber as I was leaving, "but I got you something for Christmas."

She smiled at me.

I absolutely *loved* that smile.

"Sorry it's not wrapped," I said, pulling a book out and giving it to her. "Have you ever read this?"

It was C. S. Lewis' *The Magician's Nephew*. Amber looked at it and shook her head.

"Well," I explained, "there are seven of these . . . just like the Harry Potter books. So, if you read this over break and you like it, I'll get you the other ones, okay?"

She nodded and signed, *Thank you.*

"Can you tell me?" I asked her, leaning forward.

She nodded and set the book down so she could cup her hands around my ear to say it.

"Merry Christmas," I said, giving her a hug when she was done.

She whispered into her cupped hands one more time.

"Merry Christmas."

"So, do I even want to know what you and Tanner did last night?" Laci asked when I got back from the school.

"Probably not," I said, not volunteering anything else. Somehow I had the feeling that Laci wasn't going to see quite so clearly just how *right* I was.

She shook her head and didn't ask any more questions.

"Do you have everything?" I asked her as she zipped up her suitcase.

"Probably not," she said.

That night, the kids and I went over to have dinner with Mrs. White and Charlotte.

"When does Jordan's plane get in?" I asked Charlotte after we'd sat down. He was due to fly in the next day.

"Right after lunch."

"So, what you're saying is that I'm not gonna see you anymore after tonight?"

"If you look out your window, you might see me a few times," she grinned. (Jordan and his mom lived across the street from me and Laci.)

"Oh, goody," I said.

"Are you and Jordan going to get married?" Dorito asked.

"Maybe," Charlotte said, still smiling.

"And what will that make me?" he asked.

"What?"

"You know," I explained. "When someone marries your sister then they're your "brother-in-law" . . .""

"Oh," Charlotte nodded. "Well, let's see. I guess since your dad acts like he's my dad too, that would make you my brother, so you would be Jordan's brother-in-law."

"Really?" he asked happily.

"No," I said. "I don't act like her *dad*. I act like her brother. Her young, cool, hip brother."

Charlotte suppressed a laugh and Mrs. White smiled.

"So, what would that make me?" Dorito wanted to know.

"Well," I said. "Since Charlotte is like my sister, you're like her nephew. So Jordan would be your uncle."

"Cool!" Dorito said. "Just like Uncle Tanner!"

"Sure," I said.

"He's gonna be so messed up," Charlotte muttered.

"So do you and "Uncle Jordan" have big plans for the next two weeks?" I asked.

104

"Nothing too big," she said. "We're supposed to go skiing on Friday, but other than that, we're just gonna hang out . . . do family stuff, you know."

"Family stuff?"

"You know, Christmas here, Christmas there." She stuffed a forkful of salad in her mouth.

"We're still doing Christmas Eve here, right?" I asked.

"I'm planning on it," Mrs. White said.

"Christmas!" Dorito said, holding his fork high up in the air.

"Christmas!" Lily said, clapping.

"And then are you doing Christmas morning at their house?"

"I dunno," she said, shrugging and wiping her mouth. "I don't think they really know what they're doing yet."

"How come?" Mrs. White asked.

"Chase is talking about not coming home for Christmas."

"Why not?"

"I dunno," she said again. "He said he's having trouble with his truck and he doesn't think he's gonna be able to make it."

"Oh," Mrs. White said. "That's a shame. I know Jordan will be disappointed if he doesn't get to see Chase."

"We'll see him," Charlotte said, taking a drink of milk. "If Chase can't make it here, we'll probably take their mom up there and go see him. We might even try to surprise him. I just don't know when we're gonna go."

Uh-oh, I thought. *This is* not *going to turn out well.*

After I got the kids in bed I checked my cell phone, which I had accidentally left on my dresser when I'd gone over to the White's. There was one missed call from my mom. I looked at the time and decided it was too late to call her on a school night, so I decided I'd try her back tomorrow after she was through teaching. I figured I knew what she wanted anyway – I had completely forgotten to get those boxes out of my room over the weekend.

Wednesday evening there was a fellowship dinner at church. After that, Lily and I sat in the sanctuary and watched Dorito and the other kids practice for the Christmas pageant.

When we got home I put the kids to bed and I called Mom.

"I saw you called last night," I said. "Sorry I didn't answer. I didn't have my phone with me."

"Oh," she said. "Don't worry about it."

"You didn't leave a message and I was afraid you were already in bed . . ."

"That's okay," she said, sounding distracted. "It's doesn't matter now."

"You guys wanna go out for dinner tomorrow night?" I asked. What I was actually hoping for was an invitation to another home cooked meal, but what I wound up getting was nothing.

"I'm sorry, honey," she said. "We're busy."

"Doing what?"

"Maybe we could get together over the weekend," she answered.

"Okay," I said. "But what are you guys doing?"

"Now's not a good time, David," she said. "I really need to go."

"Okay," I said, mildly puzzled, and I hung up the phone.

I called Laci next.

"So where are you gonna take the kids tomorrow night?" she asked when I told her about my conversation with my mom.

"Maybe I'm gonna cook!"

"Yeah, right!"

"I could!"

"But you won't," she laughed.

"Probably not."

"Why don't you call my mom?" Laci suggested.

"No," I said. "She's already watching Lily for me three days this week. I don't need her to cook for me too."

"She doesn't mind."

106

"I know," I said. "But we'll just go to Chuck E. Cheese's. Dorito's been bugging me to go there."

"That's awfully loud for Lily," Laci worried.

"She'll be fine," I said. "I promise."

"Don't forget he's got Scouts!"

"I won't," I said. "That's gonna be my excuse to get him out of there!"

"Okay. Well, have fun."

"Oh, I'm sure we will."

"I miss you," she said.

"I miss you, too."

"I love you."

"I love you, too."

The next morning I dropped Dorito off at school and then took Lily by Laci's parents'.

"You sure you three don't want to come over for dinner tonight?" Laci's mom asked.

"Laci told you to invite me?"

"She said something about saving you from Chuck E. Cheese's," she laughed.

"Too late," I said, shaking my head. "I already promised Dorito."

"Ahhh," she said, knowingly. "He remembers I'm picking him up from school again today, right?"

"Yep. He's very excited about it."

"Good."

"As a matter of fact, if you want to try and talk him into coming over here for dinner . . ."

"I don't think I stand a chance against Chuck E. Cheese's."

"Probably not," I admitted.

"But, I have an idea," she said. "Why don't the four of you come over tomorrow night? You know Laci's not going to feel like cooking when she gets home and you probably aren't going to want to go out again."

"Are you sure? You've done a lot already."

"Absolutely. And that'll give us a chance to find out all about her trip, too."

"That sounds great. Thanks."

I gave Lily a hug and kissed her goodbye.

"I'll be back before dinner, all right?" I asked her. She nodded.

"And then we'll go to see the big mouse, okay?"

"Mouse," she said, clapping her hands.

"That's right," I said. "You be good for Grandma. I'll see you tonight."

It was about four-thirty that afternoon when I heard the front door slam open.

"David?!" I heard Charlotte hollering.

"Up here," I called back. I could hear her stomping up the stairs and I twirled around in my chair just in time to see her storm through my office door. She glared at me.

"What?"

"How long have you known?" Her voice was quiet, but angry. Her face was streaked with tears.

"Charlotte," I said, tilting my head at her sympathetically.

"HOW LONG?"

I took a deep breath.

"Since August," I finally said quietly. She shook her head at me in disgust and stomped back down the hall.

"Charlotte, wait!" I jumped out of my chair and raced after her. By the time I got to her she was already at the front door and I grabbed her by the arm. She pulled away and glared at me.

"I will never forgive you for this, David. *Never.*"

"Tanner made me promise I wouldn't say anything."

"Don't even *talk* to me about Tanner!"

"Come on, Charlotte . . ."

"No, David," she yelled. "You *come on*! I thought I could *trust* you! How could you keep something like this from me?"

"Charlotte, I—"

"You know what, David?" she asked, opening the door. "I don't even want to hear it."

She stormed out before I could say another word and climbed into her car, which was parked in Jordan's driveway. She slammed the door, started the car and raced away. After she was gone, I noticed that Tanner's truck was in the driveway too. I walked over and knocked on the door.

"So, I gather Jordan found out?" I said when Tanner answered the door.

"Yeah," Tanner sighed, letting me in.

"Thanks a lot for the warning . . ."

"Sorry," he said. "Charlotte mad at you?"

I glared at him.

"Sorry," he said again.

"How's Jordan?"

"Okay. I think mostly he's worried about Chase right now."

"That figures," I said.

Tanner nodded.

"Hi, David," Jordan said, emerging from the kitchen with a package of cookies.

"Hi."

"You want some Oreos?" he asked.

"Are they Double Stuf?"

"Of course . . ."

"Got any milk?"

He put the package on the coffee table and went back for a gallon of milk and three cups.

"So, Charlotte really let you have it, huh?" Jordan asked, pouring some milk into a cup and sliding it toward me.

I nodded.

"She'll get over it."

"I don't think so . . ."

"Yes, she will," he assured me. "She's just upset right now, and she needed someone to take it out on. You know how she is."

I sighed and twisted the top off of a cookie.

"It's actually quite a compliment," Jordan smiled.

"How do you figure that?" Tanner asked.

"She knows that he's safe," Jordan explained, then he looked at me. "She knows she can say anything she wants to you and you'll still be there for her."

"So, what you're saying is that I should be feeling really, really *good* right now?"

"Absolutely," he grinned. "You're very special to Charlotte."

I sighed again. "Lucky, lucky me."

We sat for a few moments quietly dunking Oreos into milk.

"You gonna get tested?" I finally asked, breaking the silence.

"I dunno yet," he shrugged. "I haven't had a lot of time to think about it yet. I just found out."

"I'm sorry."

"It'll be all right," he promised, taking another cookie out of the pack. "No matter what, it'll be all right."

Charlotte came back at two in the morning and woke me up by rapping persistently on the storm door. I flipped on the front porch light, saw who it was, and opened the door.

"What's the matter?" I asked. "Kinda hard to barge in when the door's locked?"

She burst into tears. I pulled her inside and led her over to the couch.

"I don't want this to be happening," she sobbed after we sat down.

"I know," I said, putting my arm around her and rubbing her shoulder. "I'm sorry."

"What are we gonna do?" she cried.

"I . . . I don't know," I admitted.

"I thought everything was finally . . . *good*, you know? That everything was finally going to be okay."

"You don't even know if he's got it or not," I said. "Everything might be fine."

"And what if it's not fine? What if he's got it?"

"Then . . . then we'll all get through it together somehow."

"And Chase isn't going to be fine," she cried.

"I know," I said quietly. I squeezed her and kissed the top of her head.

I really wished Laci was there. She was so much better at this stuff than I was.

What would Laci say if she were here?

"Charlotte," I said after a moment, "all I know is that it isn't really about *us*. It's about *God*, and He has this perfect plan that He's in control of and we're a part of it. Sometimes we understand what He's doing . . . sometimes we don't."

She buried her head against me for another minute and didn't say anything. Then, she finally sat back a bit.

"I'm sorry I took it out on you earlier," she said, wiping her tears on her sleeve.

"It's okay."

"I just needed someone to yell at," she went on.

"You can yell at me anytime you need to," I smiled.

"Thanks," she said, sniffing and giving me a small smile back.

"It's going to be okay," I said, tucking a strand of hair behind her ear. "No matter what, it's going to be okay."

She leaned back, let out a ragged breath, and rested her head against the couch.

"You know," Charlotte said quietly after a moment, "most kids my age have normal lives."

"You've been through a lot," I agreed.

"So why can't God just let me be normal now for a while – you know? I just wanna go to school, be with Jordan, get married one day, have kids . . . just *normal* stuff."

"Normal's overrated," I said.

"I wouldn't know."

She didn't say anything else for a few moments, and neither did I.

"What if Jordan *dies?*" she finally asked in a terrified whisper, breaking the silence.

"Have you talked to Jordan about it?" I finally asked her.

She shook her head. "Not yet."

"You know what I bet Jordan would say? I bet he'd say that whatever glorifies God the most is what he wants to have happen."

"I know he would." She sniffed and wiped her eyes again. Then, more quietly, she said, "But I'm not there yet."

She let out another ragged sigh and rested her head on my shoulder.

"Greg was a lot like Jordan," I told her after a minute.

"He was?"

"Uh-huh. He always put God first."

"Oh," she paused for a long moment, then finally said, "I really don't remember much."

"What do you mean?"

"I mean about my dad and Greg . . . I really don't remember very much about them."

"Oh."

We sat quietly for a little while, and for a minute I thought maybe she'd fallen asleep.

"Nice tattoo," she said, admiring the back of my hand.

"Thanks."

"Is it a princess?"

"No."

"Yes it is," she argued.

"Lily picked it out."

"Uh-huh. Sure she did."

"She did."

"Dave?" she asked after a few moments.

"What?"

"Will you tell me about them?"

"About your dad and Greg?"

"Uh-huh."

"Sure," I said. "What do you wanna know?"

"Everything."

~ ~ ~

I WOKE UP the next morning to what would turn out to be the longest day of my entire life. It started with Dorito jumping into my bed with me and bouncing up and down.

"Guess what?!" he asked when he saw me peer at him through one eye.

"Charlotte's on the couch?"

"YES!" he cried, bouncing higher.

"I'm surprised you didn't wake her up."

"She told me to go away," he explained.

"Ahhh," I nodded. "Stop bouncing."

"How come it's light out already?" Dorito asked.

I looked at the clock and groaned.

"You're gonna be late for school," I told him.

"I wanna stay here and play with Charlotte!" he protested.

"Nope. One more day of school and then you get to stay home for two weeks."

He looked at me doubtfully.

"Plus, today's your class party. You don't wanna miss that, do you?"

He sighed. "Well, can Charlotte spend the night again?"

"Charlotte can sleep on the couch anytime she wants," I promised.

This satisfied him and he trundled off to his room to get dressed while I went to the kitchen and found a pack of Pop-Tarts for him to eat in the car.

"Charlotte!" I said, pulling on my coat.

"Mmm."

"Charlotte!" I said again, swatting her on the head with a glove. "Wake up!"

"What?"

"I've gotta run Dorito to school. You're in charge of Lily."

"Where is she?" Charlotte asked, not opening her eyes.

114

"She's still sleeping."

"And so you're waking me up *why?*"

"So you'll know you're in charge."

"Whatever," she said, turning over and nestling back down into the couch.

Lily and Charlotte were both still sleeping when I got back, so I went into the kitchen and poured myself some cereal. I was almost done eating when Lily started cooing in her bedroom. I quickly shoveled down the last few spoonfuls of cereal and was putting the bowl in the sink when the doorbell rang. It was Jordan.

"I saw Charlotte's car in your driveway. Is she here?" he asked.

I nodded. He looked over my shoulder into the living room and smiled.

"See," he said, looking back at me. "I told you that you were very special to her!"

I rolled my eyes at him.

"A bunch of us are going skiing," he explained, striding toward the couch. "She was supposed to meet me twenty minutes ago."

"Hey, Charlotte," he said, gently shaking her shoulder. "Wake up."

Funny how she woke right up for *Jordan*.

"Hey," she smiled at him, reaching up and hugging him.

"Good morning," he smiled, hugging her back. "We've gotta get going or we're gonna be late."

"I look awful," Charlotte moaned.

"No, you don't," Jordan told her. "You look beautiful."

"And THAT, my friends," I said, heading toward Lily's room, "is what they mean when they say 'Love is blind'!"

After Charlotte and Jordan left, I took Lily to her weekly Mother's Morning Out at our church and reminded her that Grandma was going to pick her up.

When I got home, I was surprised to find Tanner sitting in the living room waiting for me.

"Hey, what's up?" I asked him. "Don't you have school today?"

"Today's make-up exams," he explained. "I'm done."

Then he asked, "When's Laci coming home?"

"Her plane comes in in about four hours. Why?"

"I, uh, I found out something about Anthony."

"What?"

Tanner ran his hand over the top of his head.

"He, um, he really shouldn't be in the same house with Amber."

"Why?" I cried. "What did you find out?"

"I don't know how to say this," Tanner said. "He's a really messed-up kid."

"Messed-up, how?"

"He got taken away from his mom when he was about seven years old. He got taken out of his house because his mom's boyfriend was . . ."

"Was what?" I asked when he didn't go on.

"Was molesting him," Tanner finally said, reluctantly.

"How'd you find that out?"

"I can't tell you."

"Okay," I said slowly, "but why'd you say that he shouldn't be in the same house with Amber?"

"It's really common for kids who've been abused like that to become abusers themselves," Tanner said. I felt my stomach tighten.

"But they don't *all* become abusers, do they?" I asked in a panicky voice. "Just because he was abused doesn't mean that he–"

"He did," Tanner interrupted.

"What?"

"He did become an abuser."

"What?"

"I'm telling you that he molested a little kid and that he doesn't need to be in that house with Amber."

"Are you sure about this?"

"Yes."

116

"How do you know for sure?"

"I *know*," he said, emphatically.

"Does Social Services know?" I cried.

"I don't know. I guess not."

"I mean, they . . . they surely wouldn't put Amber in a home with someone who has sexually abused kids if they knew about it . . . would they?"

"I don't know how she got put in the same house with him," Tanner said.

"We've gotta call them and let them know!" I said, lifting my phone from my belt.

"No!" Tanner said, stopping me. "David, listen to me! We can't tell anybody."

"We have to!"

"No," he said again. "We can't let anybody know that we know about this."

"But—"

"Look, a friend went way out on a limb to get me this information," Tanner said. "They could lose their job."

"I don't really care about some friend of yours and their *job* right now!"

"They're not just my friend," he said quietly. "They're a friend of yours, too." I stared at him. "And it's about more than just them losing their job . . . they could go to jail."

"Who is it?"

"I'm not going to tell you, but I promise you don't want them to go to jail."

"We have to get Amber out of there!" I finally said, turning back to him.

"We will."

"How? What are we going to do?"

"Don't worry," Tanner assured me. "I've got a plan."

~ ~ ~

AFTER TANNER LEFT, I called Amber's social worker. I couldn't help myself. She didn't answer her phone, but I left a message.

"This is David Holland," I said. "I need to talk with you about something . . . something very important. Please call me back as soon as you get this message."

After that I was way too uptight to get any work done. I decided I'd better go to Mom and Dad's and get the rest of my stuff since I'd promised them everything would be out of there four days ago.

I prayed the entire way over to Mom and Dad's.

Please, Lord, keep Amber safe. Please, God, help me and Tanner to get Amber out of that house. Please don't let anything happen to her.

~ ~ ~

I HAD JUST pulled into my parent's driveway and turned the car off when my phone rang.

"Hello?"

"Mr. Holland?"

"Yes?"

"This is Erin Lamont, returning your call."

"Oh, yes," I said, my heart pounding in my chest. "Thank you for calling me back."

"What can I do for you?" she asked, sounding like she didn't really want to know.

"What do you know about the older boy who's living there with Amber?"

"Mr. Holland," she sighed. "I've told you . . . I cannot discuss any specifics of the children who are under our supervision."

"Do you know anything about him?" I persisted.

"I'm not going to discuss this with you."

"Amber needs to be out of that house!" I practically shouted.

"It is the policy of the Department of Children's Welfare to not remove a child from a certified foster home without justification–"

"But there *is* justification," I argued.

"Such as?"

"The older boy in that family . . . he's not the kind of person Amber needs to be around! It can't be good for Amber to be living in the same house with him. Who knows what he's–"

"I know that you want Amber," she interrupted. "I understand that. But all of our families – *and all members of those families* – have undergone rigorous background checks, home studies, and trainings. I can assure you that we do not place children in a home unless we are confident they will be safe and well cared for."

"She is NOT safe in that home," I insisted.

"Do you have any more "evidence" of wrongdoing on the part of this boy or the family?"

Tanner's voice rang in my head. *David, listen to me! We can't tell anybody . . .*

"Well, no," I stammered, "but—"

"Quite frankly, Mr. Holland, Amber's placement is none of your business," she said. "I don't know how much more clear I can make that to you."

"Could you just investigate this boy?" I begged.

"I have TOLD you, Mr. Holland. All of the families that we place children with have been thoroughly—"

"NOT THIS TIME!" I yelled into the phone. "Why can't you just admit that maybe you made a mistake? I'm telling you that somebody needs to investigate that boy that's living there. It's your *job* to make sure that Amber's safe."

"You do not need to tell me how to do my job."

"Somebody does," I said, still yelling, "because obviously you're not doing it!"

I was desperate.

"If I have to," I threatened, "I'll call your supervisor and make sure Amber's removed from that home!"

There was a pause before she responded.

"Mr. Holland," she said, rather sweetly, "my biggest concern for Amber at this moment, actually, is that a grown man who barely knows her and who has no apparent reason for involving himself in her life to the extent that you have, has developed an abnormal and questionable interest in her. Frankly, I find that your continual investigation into every aspect of Amber's life is not only disturbing, but quite possibly I believe it could be considered stalking, which – as I'm sure you're aware – is illegal in this state.

"I'm afraid, Mr. Holland," she went on, "that if you don't stop obsessing over this child, then I'll have no other choice but to file a restraining order against you."

"You wouldn't dare . . ."

"Don't kid yourself, Mr. Holland," she said, her voice suddenly cold. "I file restraining orders against people all the time if I feel they're a threat to the children I supervise. It's my *job*. You won't be

120

allowed to get within two hundred yards of her . . . not even to walk your little boy into his classroom in the morning.

"Now," she said, once again in that sickly sweet tone. "Is there anything else that you need to discuss with me, or can I get back to my *job?*"

I was speechless.

"I gather we're done then, Mr. Holland," she said when I didn't answer. "Have a good day."

And then she hung up.

~ ~ ~

I SAT FOR a moment in disbelief. I closed my phone and stared out the window to my parent's house. Finally, I looked at my watch.

Dad was probably going to arrive any minute – he usually came home around eleven for lunch. I decided to try and get my things fast and get out of there before he showed up. My stomach was too knotted up to make small talk right now.

I let myself in through the front door quickly and bounded up the steps. Once I reached the top step I hurried down the hall, but what I saw when I stepped into my bedroom made me stop in my tracks.

The boxes that I'd stacked so neatly in my closet a few weeks before were now along the wall, under the window. Some of the boxes were opened and some of the stuff was out of them.

But more than that. Apparently Mom and Dad's "guest" had arrived.

He was sitting in front of those opened boxes – in the midst of all my things – and he was looking at my yearbook. He was reading the page that had been dedicated to Greg and Mr. White. The page with the message on it that I'd written to them.

"Hey," he said. "Look what I found."

He turned toward me a bit to show me the yearbook. I could see his face now. He was smiling. Something about him seemed so familiar that I felt I should know him, yet I had no idea who he was.

Obviously he wasn't expecting to find me when he turned around, because his smile disappeared.

"Oh," he said, startled. "I thought you were Troy."

(Troy was my dad.)

"What are you doing?" I yelled.

"N-n-nothing," he stammered.

"You are too! Get outta my stuff!"

"I'm . . . I'm sorry," he said, standing up and extending a hand toward me. "I'm Jacob."

122

"I don't give a rip WHO you are!" I said.

Except that I didn't really say "rip".

I said a word that I only say on days when I've found out that a little girl I love is probably being molested and that there's nothing I can do about it. Something I say only on days when someone threatens to take out a restraining order against me. Only on days that Jordan might have a devastating neurological disease. And only on days that I walk into my old bedroom and find a stranger searching through my most personal belongings.

"Get outta my stuff!" I yelled, stalking over to him and trying to grab the yearbook out of his hands. It tumbled to the floor and landed face down, pages bending.

"Now look what you did!" I said, still yelling. "You ruined it!"

"You did that!" he argued. "I didn't do it."

"If you hadn't been messing with all my stuff in the first place it wouldn't have happened," I said, kneeling down next to the yearbook and trying to straighten out the pages. I closed the cover and put it into an opened box.

That's when I saw Greg's sweatshirt. On the floor.

Greg had worn that sweatshirt the last time we'd played one-on-one in our driveway a few days before he'd died. It had been unusually warm that day and he'd stripped it off, hanging it over the fence and playing in just his t-shirt. He'd forgotten to grab it before he went home, and Mom had washed it so it would be clean when I gave it back to him . . . but I'd never had the chance.

Now I reached for it – to get it off the floor. To fold it carefully and put it on top of the yearbook – where it belonged.

"Let me help," Jacob said, grabbing it just before I did and carelessly stuffing it into another open box.

"Quit touching my stuff!" I yelled, shoving him away from the boxes, hard. He sprawled backwards and I grabbed the sweatshirt.

Jacob rose to his feet and came after me. I'd just managed to get to my feet when he slugged me in the jaw. Now I was the one who went sprawling backwards across the floor. My head hit the wall and I literally saw stars.

I scrambled to my feet and headed back toward him, ready to punch him back, but before I could, someone grabbed me from behind and stopped me.

"David!"

It was my father. I turned to face him, lowering my fists.

"What in the world is going on here?" he asked.

"I came over here to get the rest of my stuff," I cried "and I found this . . . this *stranger* going through all of my things!"

"Jacob," my dad asked. "Are you okay?"

Jacob nodded.

Dad loosened his grip.

"Jacob, this is my son, David. I'm sorry if he was rude to you—"

"You're sorry if *I* was rude to *him?*" I yelled, shrugging Dad's hand off of my arm.

I couldn't believe it.

"Jacob is a *guest* in this home," Dad began firmly, but I didn't stick around to let him finish.

I turned and snatched up the sweatshirt and the yearbook and then I stalked out of the room, ignoring the sounds of my dad, who was calling after me.

~ ~ ~

I DIDN'T ANSWER the phone either time that Dad called as I drove the two blocks to Mrs. White's house. I could see through the garage window that her car was there, so I rang the doorbell.

"Hi!" Mrs. White smiled when she opened the door. I did my best to smile back. "This is a nice surprise."

I nodded.

"What's wrong?" she asked. I couldn't answer. I just gave my head the slightest of shakes and looked away.

"Come in," she said, and I obeyed. We walked over to the couch and sat down.

"What do you have there?" she asked, pointing to the sweatshirt in my hand.

"Oh, um, this was Greg's. I was going through some stuff in my old bedroom and I found it. I thought you might want it."

She took it from me and held it out in front of her.

"Oh, goodness," she said. "I remember this! He got it one of the times Paul took you guys to Chicago, didn't he?"

I nodded. Paul was Mr. White, but I could never bring myself to call him anything except Mr. White.

"You can keep it if you want," she offered, extending it back toward me. "You're the one that went on those trips."

"Are you sure?" I asked.

"Sure, I'm sure."

"Thanks," I said, taking it from her and trying to give her a smile.

"Charlotte told me about Chase," she said, obviously assuming that's what I was so upset about.

I nodded.

"It seems like that family's been through so much lately."

I nodded again.

"That's not all that's wrong," she said, looking at me questioningly.

"There's so much wrong," I said, shaking my head again. "I don't even know where to begin."

She didn't ask me any more questions. She just sat quietly until I was ready to talk.

"Did you know that my parents let somebody move in?" I finally blurted. "Some guy they don't even know is living in my bedroom?"

"Yes," she nodded, looking at me sympathetically. "I know."

"I went over there and caught him pawing through all of my stuff, helping himself to whatever he wanted!"

"What?"

"I went over there to get some boxes, and he was going through all of my stuff . . . like he owned it or something!"

"He was helping himself to whatever he wanted?" she asked.

"He, well . . . he had my stuff out. He was looking at it."

"But he wasn't *taking* anything?"

"Who knows what he would have done if I hadn't of come along?"

"Looking at your stuff isn't exactly the same as taking things."

"Anybody who would violate someone's privacy like that is pretty much capable of anything if you ask me," I told her.

"David," she said, tilting her head and looking at me doubtfully.

"What!?"

"What was he looking at?" she asked.

"Are you defending him now or something? It doesn't matter what he was looking at! He shouldn't have been going through my stuff!"

"No, maybe he shouldn't have been. I was just wondering what he was looking at."

"My yearbook," I said quietly after a moment.

She looked at me doubtfully again and I could tell she was wondering what was so private about a yearbook that had been purchased by over twelve hundred students.

"It was *private*," I insisted. "Okay?"

"Okay," she agreed, "but, David–"

"He also punched me," I told her.

126

"What?"

"Yeah," I nodded, showing her my jaw. "He slugged me right here!"

"I can't believe Jacob would do that!" she said, reaching out and touching my jaw.

"You *know* him?" I asked, incredulous.

"Do you want some ice?" she asked.

"How do you know him?"

"I met him Wednesday when he moved in."

"You honestly think this is a good idea for my parents to have some stranger living in their house when he obviously can't be trusted?"

"I think he can be trusted," Mrs. White said.

"He was pawing through all of my stuff and he punched me!" I reminded her.

"I think maybe you two must have just gotten off on the wrong foot."

"I can't believe you're taking his side!"

"I'm not taking anybody's side," she said. "I just think that—"

"I mean, someone at church says they know someone who needs a place to stay and suddenly my parents decide they're a Ramada Inn? How is that a smart thing to do?"

She looked at me for a long moment and then sighed.

"David," she finally said, "there's something you need to know."

"What?"

"I need to tell you something." She sighed again. "You're going to find out soon enough anyway."

"What?" I asked again.

She leaned back and took a deep breath.

"What's going on?"

"David," she said, still looking at me and giving me a little smile. "Paul always thought a lot of you."

"I always thought a lot of him too," I said, smiling back.

"I know you did," she nodded. "And he knew it, too. He knew that you and Greg looked up to him, and it was really important to him that he set a good example for both of you."

"He did," I said. "The best. As a matter of fact, the only reason I'm even leading that stupid youth group is because he did such a good job with ours . . ."

She smiled again.

"Listen, David," she said, glancing away for a moment as if trying to decide what to say next. "You know that everybody makes mistakes . . . sometimes we do things that we regret later and wish we hadn't of done."

"Sure," I agreed.

"And," she went on, "when you're a parent, sometimes you may not exactly want your kids to know everything that you've done . . . right?"

I nodded.

"It's not that you want to lie to them or anything," she explained hurriedly, "but you also don't exactly want to brag about it either. They might think, 'Oh, well, Dad used to smoke cigarettes, so it's okay if I do too.' Even if you've told them it was a mistake and that it's *not* okay, there's this unspoken message that since Mom or Dad did something, it somehow is okay. Do you understand what I mean?"

"Mr. White used to smoke?"

She sighed.

"No, David. I'm not talking about cigarettes."

"Pot?"

"No, not pot. Well, actually, he probably *did* smoke pot and cigarettes, but that's not what I'm trying to get at here at all."

Mr. White smoked pot and cigarettes?

"What *are* you trying to get at?" I asked.

She hesitated.

"Don't worry," I told her, trying to pull myself together and making sure my mouth wasn't hanging open in dismay. "You're not

128

going to tell me anything that's going to change how I felt about him."

And as I said those words, I realized that they were true. She smiled at me and nodded.

"I didn't meet Paul until my junior year in college," she said. "He was a senior, but I'd never seen him before. One night he showed up at one of our Campus Crusade for Christ meetings and . . ."

She paused.

"Love at first sight?" I guessed.

"Well, maybe not love at first sight," she smiled, "but it was close."

I smiled back at her.

"He had just accepted Christ," she explained. "And he was just so . . . so *on fire*. You know what I mean?"

I nodded.

"But before that," she went on, "I'm afraid he spent the first three years of college, um . . ."

"Sowing his wild oats?" I suggested.

"Yeah, whatever that means," she laughed. Then she turned serious.

"I . . . I wasn't Paul's first girlfriend."

"Okay."

"I mean . . . I'm afraid he didn't exactly *save* himself for me. Do you know what I mean?"

"Uh-huh," I nodded. For the first time in this whole conversation, I think I actually *did* know what she meant. "But why are you telling me all this?"

"He had a girlfriend before he met me," she said. "Her name was Olivia."

"Okay," I said slowly.

"They broke up after he accepted Christ. You know . . . different values, all that sort of thing."

I nodded.

"He never saw her again after we started dating. Never even knew what became of her."

I looked at her, confused again.

"David," she sighed, "Olivia never told him, but . . . she was pregnant when they broke up."

"Pregnant?"

"With his baby."

I felt my eyes widen.

"Olivia went away," she explained, "and had the baby and never told Paul. He never knew."

"When did he find out?" I asked.

"He *never* found out," she said. "Paul died thinking he had no other children except for Greg and Charlotte. He never knew about the baby."

"How do you know about it then?" I asked, not even *close* to figuring this out on my own.

She gave me a little smile and looked at me gently.

"Because that baby's all grown up now," she explained, putting a hand on mine. "And he's sitting in your old bedroom right now, pawing through all of your stuff."

~ ~ ~

I SHOOK MY head.

"What?"

She nodded.

"No," I said, still shaking my head. "There's no way that guy is . . ."

"Yes," she said when I hesitated. "He's Paul's son. And he's Greg and Charlotte's half-brother."

Half-brother.

"There's got to be some kind of mistake," I said, still shaking my head. "Something's not right. How'd you even find out about him?"

"He found me," she explained. "His mother was able to give him enough information about Paul that he was able to track me down."

"How do you know Mr. White's really his father?" I asked. "She could have slept with a hundred other guys."

"Didn't he look familiar to you?" she asked gently. I remembered how he'd turned and smiled at me when I'd first walked into my old room. It had been Greg's smile . . . Charlotte's smile. The truth of what she was saying made me stop shaking my head.

I stared at her.

"What's he want?" I finally asked. "Money? He found out about Charlotte's trust fund and now he thinks he'll just come right in here and help himself?"

"No," she said, shaking her head. "That's not what he wants."

"You need to get yourself a lawyer and—"

"David!" she interrupted. "He's not after the money. That's not why he found us."

"Us?"

"Me and Charlotte."

"*Charlotte knows?*"

"No," she answered.

I breathed a sigh of relief.

"She doesn't know yet," Mrs. White explained.

"*Yet?*" I practically shouted. "You're not honestly considering letting Charlotte find out about this, are you?"

"*She's his sister!*"

"HALF–sister," I corrected. "Do you really think anything good's gonna come out of her finding out that she's related to that low-life?"

"He's sick, David."

"Tell me about it."

"No. I mean . . . physically. He's very sick. He needs a bone marrow transplant."

I stared at her, and suddenly everything became crystal clear.

"No, no, no," I said, shaking my head again. "A bone marrow transplant? From Charlotte? Are you *kidding* me?"

"If he can find a donor, his chances for survival increase tremendously."

"Then tell him to go to that national registry thingy and find a donor there!"

"They've already looked on the national registry and there were no perfect matches. There were three people who matched five out of six markers and they can use one of those if they have to, but it would be much better if they can find a perfect match.

"There's only a small chance that Charlotte's going to be a match because they're only half-siblings," she went on, "but Jacob's doctors felt it was worth pursuing. That's why Olivia gave him the information he needed to find us."

I rubbed my forehead and looked at Mrs. White.

"When are you going to tell her?" I asked.

"I was going to tell her tonight after she gets back from skiing."

"Is she going to meet him?"

"As long as she wants to. That's the main reason he's here."

"So this isn't just about him being sick. He wants to meet her."

"Of course he does! If you had a sister you never knew about, wouldn't you want to meet her?"

"*Half*-sister," I corrected.

132

"Wouldn't you?"

"I don't know," I shrugged.

"Well, I know," she said. "You'd want to. And he wants to. And I expect that Charlotte's going to want to as well."

Laci listened on the car ride back from the airport with her hand clapped over her mouth most of the time, her eyes wide.

"I cannot believe Charlotte has a brother!" she finally said when I finished.

"*Half*-brother."

"Does he look like Greg? I wanna meet him!!"

"No, you don't," I assured her. "He's nothing like Greg."

"You talked with him for what . . . five minutes?" she asked. "How could you possibly know anything about him?"

"He punched me!" I said.

"Yeah," she argued. "After you pushed him."

"You don't want to meet him. Trust me."

"I can't believe Greg has a brother," she whispered, completely awed.

"A *half*-brother! How many times do I have to say that?!"

"Mr. White had another son. This is unbelievable!"

"What's unbelievable, Laci, is that you're getting so excited about this. I'm telling you that Charlotte is going to wind up getting hurt here. Nobody seems to be thinking about her, except for me."

"What are you talking about?"

"He's not . . . he's not the kind of person you'd really want to be related to. This is someone who . . . who's going to be nothing but a burden to her! Maybe for the rest of her life! She'd be better off if she never even knew about him."

"Well," Laci said, "she's going to find out about him. I don't think that you need to let this ruin your day."

"Oh, that's not the only thing that's ruining my day."

"What else happened?" she asked.

"Nothing," I muttered. I couldn't bring myself to tell her about Amber just yet.

"Tanner and I are going to go do something tonight," I said.

"*Tonight?*" she asked.

"I know you just got back," I said, "but it's really important."

"But what about dinner? My mom's cooking for us!"

"Can you take the kids and go without me?" I asked. "Please? It's really important."

"What are you doing?" she asked.

I glanced at her.

"This isn't a good idea, David," she said when I didn't answer.

"You don't even know what we're going to do!" I protested.

"I know it's not a good idea!"

"You're probably right," I had to agree.

I was so mad at my dad and Jacob and Erin Lamont that by the time Tanner picked me up that evening, I was feeling reckless.

"Hello, Tanner," Laci said ruefully when she let him in the door. He stepped into the living room and she inspected him. Like me, he was dressed in dark clothing. Unlike me, he had black grease smeared under each eye.

"You look ridiculous," she said, glaring at him.

"Well, you're in a fine mood this evening," he observed. "Jet lag?"

"No," she said. "I just think this is a bad idea."

"You told her what we're doing?"

"No," Laci answered for me, "I just know that whatever it is, it's not a good idea and I don't appreciate the fact that you're corrupting my husband."

"*Me* corrupting *him?*" Tanner cried. "I think you've got it backwards, little missy. Your husband's the one that dragged me into this."

"Oh, yeah," I interjected. "I really had to drag you."

134

Tanner grinned at me and held a little container toward me.

"Eye black?" he asked.

"Sure," I said, taking it from him, (partly because I was feeling so reckless, but mostly because I knew it would make Laci roll her eyes). I looked in the mirror by the front door and put two black smudges under my eyes.

"How do I look?" I asked, turning around. I got the eye roll I was hoping for from Laci.

"Like a criminal," Laci answered.

"You ready?" I asked Tanner, pulling on a dark jacket.

He nodded.

"*Oorah!*"

We parked on Amber's street, a couple of doors down from her house. It was dark outside and there were lights on in the house. We sat in the truck, watching it.

"So, I called Amber's social worker today," I confessed.

"I told you *not* to do that!" Tanner cried.

"I know," I said. "It was a disaster."

"Ohhhh," Tanner groaned, leaning his forehead against the steering wheel. "What happened?"

"Don't worry, I didn't tell her anything," I assured him. "But I really screwed things up."

"How?" he asked, exasperated.

"I told her that this kid didn't belong around Amber."

Tanner glared at me.

"I didn't give her any specifics!" I insisted. "She doesn't know anything . . . *obviously.*"

"Then what happened?"

"I threatened to call her supervisor."

"Oh, brother."

"And I told her she obviously wasn't doing her job right."

"I'll bet that went over really well."

"Yeah. She's going to file a restraining order against me if I don't quit calling her about Amber."

"She threatened you with a restraining order?"

I nodded and Tanner chuckled.

"What's so funny?"

"Nothing," he said. "I just had this image of you in jail."

Now it was my turn to glare at him.

"You wouldn't last two days," he said, shaking his head.

"Thanks a lot."

"Don't worry. If things don't go well tonight, maybe we'll be cell mates. I promise I'll look out for ya."

"Thanks."

"You can be my girlfriend."

"No, thanks," I said. "So anyway, after I made Amber's caseworker so mad at me that she wants to disembowel me, guess what happened?"

"I can't imagine."

"You're right," I said. "You can't." And then I told him all about Jacob.

"You're kidding!" he exclaimed when I was finished.

I just shook my head.

"Does he look like Greg?" Tanner asked.

"Why does everybody want to know that?"

"Does he?"

"I don't know," I shrugged. "Maybe a little bit."

"Wow! I wanna meet him."

"Why don't you and Laci invite him over for tea?" I asked. "Better yet, why don't you let him move into your apartment and get him out of my old room?"

"You're a piece of work," Tanner laughed. Then he asked, "You ready to walk over there?"

"Turns out that stalking is definitely illegal in this state," I told him.

"You wanna chicken out?"

"No," I said, still feeling reckless.

136

"Then let's go."

We walked down the street and up the driveway, hopping the fence to get into the backyard. I was relieved to find that none of their outside lights had motion detectors on them – that's what I had been most afraid of.

Actually, that's not true. I had been most afraid that we wouldn't find anything . . . or maybe I was terrified that we would.

We checked out all the lower level windows again, but – like Tanner had found earlier – they were completely covered up.

It was a split level house and there was no main floor, so the only other windows were up way too high to look into. We could see that they weren't covered up as much, though, and there was a large tree in the backyard, so I hoisted myself up into it. Tanner handed the camera up to me and then pulled himself up behind me.

I put the camera strap around my neck and started climbing.

"Don't go out on that branch," Tanner insisted when he saw where I was headed. "Come right out here."

"I'm not going out on the same branch with you!" I argued. "These things were designed to hold bird's nests and squirrels, not mutant football players."

"I'm telling you," Tanner warned. "That limb's not gonna hold you."

"Refresh my memory," I said, scooting out further onto the branch. "How many years did you major in engineering?"

"Suit yourself," he mumbled. That's the last thing I remember except for the sound of my branch breaking.

To find out what happened after that, I had to rely on what I was told when I woke up in the hospital.

~ ~ ~

APPARENTLY AFTER I'D fallen to the ground in a crumpled heap, Tanner had carried me to the truck "like a knight in shining armor, rescuing a princess from a fire-breathing dragon."

My mom and Laci had enjoyed Tanner's version of the evening's events.

"And you were playing Frisbee?" Mom asked. Tanner nodded.

"In the dark?" Laci wanted to know.

"Night Frisbee," Tanner explained.

"That's the stupidest story I've ever heard," Laci said after my mom had left.

"The doctors bought it," Tanner shrugged.

"The doctors don't really care what you were doing," Laci pointed out. "For that matter, *I* don't really care what you were doing." She looked at me. "I *told* you this wasn't a good idea. I told you that from the very beginning, but nobody ever listens to me."

"I don't know what you're so mad for," I told her. "I'm the one laying here in pain."

I had broken my femur – the big, long bone in my upper thigh. The doctors had already set it and put me in a cast that ran from my groin to below my knee, but I was going to have to stay in the hospital until the next morning. Apparently, with this type of break, there was always the danger that the femoral artery had been damaged, so they were going to keep me for observation . . .

"You need some drugs," Laci said, reaching for the button that dispensed my morphine.

"No!" I said. "I can't think with that stuff in my head."

"But you're in *pain*," she reminded me.

"Can you let me talk to Tanner alone first?"

She looked hesitantly at me.

"Please?" I begged.

She glanced at Tanner and then back at me.

138

"Make him take his drugs," she told Tanner as she turned and left the room. I waited until the door shut behind her and then I looked at Tanner.

"Did you get any pictures or anything?" I asked.

"No," he said, shaking his head. "You were moaning and hollering so loud it was all I could do to get you loaded up into the truck before somebody called the cops. Besides, you busted the camera."

"And the lens?"

"Especially the lens."

"I'm sorry. I'll buy you a new one."

"Darn right, you will," Tanner smiled, except that he didn't really say "darn".

"What are we going to do?" I asked him desperately. "We've *got* to get Amber out of there!"

"I know," he said, turning serious. "I'll take care of it."

"How?"

"Let me handle it." He reached for the morphine button.

"No!" I said, trying unsuccessfully to stop him. "I want to know what you're going to do!"

"I'm going to take care of it, that's what I'm going to do."

"We've got to help her!" I said, fighting to keep my train of thought.

"I know," Tanner said again, and the room drifted away.

When I woke up some time later, I discovered that I had apparently been served lunch at some point. It sat on the TV tray next to my bed now, cold and unappetizing. I was shoving it away from me when a knock sounded at my door and Charlotte and her mom entered. Charlotte was carrying a huge balloon bouquet.

"Here," she said, giving me a quick hug before moving to tie them on the rail at the foot of the bed. "We thought these might brighten your room up a bit!"

"They do," I smiled. "Thanks."

"How are you feeling?" Mrs. White asked, also giving me a hug.

"Dandy."

"And how exactly did you do this?" she asked, looking confused. "You were playing Frisbee?"

"It's a long story," I said. "I'll fill you in some other time."

"Okay," Mrs. White agreed. "What's all that stuff under your eyes?"

"And what happened to your chin?" Charlotte asked, glancing up at me.

"I must have hit it when I fell," I told her, reaching up to rub where Jacob had hit me and glaring at Mrs. White.

"There!" Charlotte said as she finished tying the balloons and stepped back. "How's that?"

"Great," I said. "Now I can't see the TV."

"Oh!" she said. "Sorry. Let's see if I can untie them."

"No," I said. "I'm just kidding. They're fine."

She smiled. Then she moved over next to her mom and positively grinned.

"Guess what?!" she asked, beaming. "I've got a brother!"

"Yeah," I nodded. "I heard."

"You already know?" she asked, her face falling.

"I *just* found out yesterday," I explained quickly. "*Please* don't get mad at me."

She eyed me for a moment and then grinned again.

"Okay," she said. "I'll forgive you this time. Can you believe it? I mean, I just can't believe it!!"

"No," I said. "I can hardly believe it either."

"As soon as we leave here we're going over there so I can meet him!"

"You are?"

"Yeah! I'm so excited! I can't wait!"

I wondered if she had balloons for Jacob in the car.

"I wish you could come with us and meet him!" she exclaimed.

"I actually met him yesterday."

140

"You did!?"

"Yeah. Just for a minute."

"What was he like? What did you think of him?"

I cast a quick glance at Mrs. White.

"He's great," I said, looking back to Charlotte.

"Really?" Her eyes were bright and shining.

"Yeah," I nodded. "You're gonna love him."

"I can't wait!" she said again.

I nodded.

"So how long are they going to keep you in here?" Mrs. White asked.

"I'll probably get out tomorrow morning, if they decide I'm not going to bleed to death."

"Bleed to death?" Charlotte asked, worriedly.

"I'm going to be fine," I assured her.

"Maybe you can come over and have dinner with us tomorrow night!" Charlotte smiled. "I'm going to make dinner for Jacob!"

Where was my morphine button?

"Maybe," I agreed.

Charlotte's hands fidgeted and she rocked back and forth on her heels. Obviously, she could hardly wait to quit making small talk with me so she could go off and meet Jacob.

"You two don't need to hang around," I suggested. "I'm getting kinda sleepy again."

"Okay," Charlotte agreed eagerly. She started to leave, but then – as an afterthought – turned back around and gave me a quick hug and a kiss on the cheek.

"Bye!" she smiled cheerily. "See you tomorrow!"

"Bye."

Mrs. White stepped up to my bed and shook her head in a disapproving manner.

"You need to take care of yourself," she said.

"You need to take care of Charlotte," I replied quietly. "I don't like this one bit."

"Everything's going to be fine," Mrs. White assured me, leaning over my bed and kissing my forehead. "She's very happy and excited."

"Oh, really? I couldn't tell."

"Come on, Mom!" Charlotte called from the doorway.

Mrs. White smiled.

"Everything's going to be fine," she said again, patting me on the shoulder. Then, she turned and followed Charlotte out the door.

The nurse came by after they'd left.

"Where's my morphine?" I asked her.

"We weaned you off of it," she explained. "If you're still in pain, I can get you some Tylenol."

Tylenol.

"Actually, could you get me my jacket?" I asked her. It was hanging on a coat rack near the door. "I want to call someone."

"No cell phones in the hospital," she said, handing me a land line phone that was next to the bed. "You can use this, instead."

"I still need my phone," I explained. "All my numbers are in there."

"Sure," she agreed.

She handed me my jacket.

"Anything else?" she asked as I fished my phone out of the pocket. I shook my head "no."

"Turn that off as soon as you've got your numbers, okay?" she asked, pointing at my cell phone. I nodded.

After she was gone, I looked at my phone. There were no messages, no missed calls.

I picked up the room phone and called Tanner. I didn't need to look up his number – he'd had the same one ever since high school.

"Tanner, listen," I began after his voice mail picked up. "I don't know what you're doing, but I really need you to call me. I'm not supposed to use my cell phone in here and my battery's about dead

142

anyway, so call me on my room line. I'm in room 592. I really need to know what's going on. Hurry up. I'm going crazy here."

I hung up the phone and waited. By the time Laci showed up three hours later, it was dark outside and Tanner still hadn't called.

"Has Tanner called you?" I asked.

"No."

I shook my head in disgust.

"I need to talk to him!" I said. "Why hasn't he called?"

"David," she said, gently, "you need to stop this."

"I can't keep laying here doing nothing!" I protested. "I cannot believe this is happening to me! I've got to get out of here!"

"Relax, relax," she said, pushing my shoulder back down into the bed.

"I can't relax!" I said. "Amber needs me and I'm stuck here and I can't do ANYTHING and Tanner won't call me and–"

"I'll get in touch with Tanner for you, okay?" she asked.

"How?"

"I . . . I don't know," she admitted. "But after I leave here I'll get in touch with him and I'll tell him to call you, okay?"

"You promise?"

"I promise," she said, giving me a little smile.

"Well, go then," I said, waving her away with my hand.

"I'm not going to leave yet!" she protested. "I just got here!"

I sighed.

"How is your leg?" she asked.

"Itchy," I replied.

"Itchy?"

"Yeah," I said. "And I can't scratch it because of this stupid cast."

"Where does it itch?" she wanted to know.

I tapped on the cast, showing her the spot above my knee that was itching.

"I need something I can stick down there and scratch with," I explained.

"I wonder if a knitting needle would work? I think my mom has some of my grandma's old knitting stuff."

"I need something," I said. "It's driving me crazy."

"I'll see what I can find," she assured me.

"Why don't you go home now and see what you can find?" I suggested. "And see if you can get in touch with Tanner."

"I'll go in a little bit!" she argued. "I haven't seen you all day and I'm not leaving after just two minutes. Now tell me about your day."

"Charlotte and Mrs. White came by after lunch," I said, resigned to the fact that Laci wasn't going to leave until she was good and ready.

"Yeah, I know," she nodded. "They told me."

"When did you talk to them?"

"Over at your parents'."

"You went over there?"

"I wanted to meet Jacob," Laci said, giving me a little shrug.

"I can't believe you! I can't *believe* you went over there!"

"Why not?"

I shook my head with disgust.

"How was Charlotte?" I finally asked.

"She seemed great."

"Were there *balloons?*"

"Huh?"

"Nothing," I replied. "Did she seem happy?"

"Oh, she was ecstatic," Laci said, laughing. "I don't know when I've ever seen her like that before."

"So she likes him?"

"She loves him!" Laci grinned. "She thinks he's great!"

"You think he's great too?"

"What?"

"Do you think he's great, too?"

"He . . . he seemed *fine*, David. I didn't get to talk with him all that long or anything, but he seemed like a really nice guy. I think that maybe the two of you just got off on the wrong foot or–"

"You're taking his side!" I said. "I can't believe this!"

144

"I'm not taking anybody's side! There are no sides! You two just had a misunderstanding and you need to–"

"HE PUNCHED ME!" I reminded her.

"After you *pushed* him!"

"He was going through my stuff!" I argued.

"David, he was *looking* at your yearbook. He was curious about Greg. He wanted to find out more about his brother and–"

"*Half*-brother."

"Think about it, David," she said, shaking her head. "Imagine you're staying in the room of the best friend of the *half*-brother that you've never met. You want to know more about him and more about your dad and there are all these boxes in the room that you know probably have pictures in them and yearbooks and stuff. Is it really *that* unreasonable to think that you might take a look and see what's there?"

"I can't believe you're taking his side," I said, crossing my arms at her.

She let out a heavy sigh.

"Congratulations," she finally said. "You've managed to make me want to leave."

"Don't forget Tanner!" I said as she stood up and turned away.

"Uh-huh."

"Laci," I pleaded, reaching out my hand to her. "It's really important. Please."

She turned back to me and took my hand. She leaned over my bed and touched her forehead to mine.

"I promise I will get in touch with Tanner for you," she said. "I want you to get some rest and quit worrying. Please."

"And tell him to call me."

"I will."

"No matter what time it is, tell him to call me."

"Okay."

"Promise?"

"I promise," she said, kissing me. "Please try to get some rest, okay?"

I nodded.

"Don't forget," I begged as she turned again to leave.

"I won't," she said, looking back over her shoulder at me. "Get some sleep."

~ ~ ~

BETWEEN MY LEG itching and waiting for Tanner to call, sleeping was an almost impossible mission. I drifted off once, jolting awake from a nightmare in which Amber was looking out a window, banging on the glass, calling for me. I was lying on the ground below with my leg twisted grotesquely under my body, unable to move. I tried to call back to her, but my voice wouldn't work.

"Would you like something to help you sleep?" the nurse asked when she checked on me in the middle of the night. I shook my head, afraid that if she gave me something, I wouldn't wake up when Tanner called.

If Tanner called.

I fell asleep again, this time waking from a dream that Jacob and Charlotte were going to Disney World together. They would have invited me along, but they were going to rent a Corvette and drive all the way to Florida. There simply wasn't going to be enough room for me and my cast.

I was fuming by the time Laci picked me up in the morning.

"You promised me you'd get in touch with Tanner!" I said as soon as she walked in the door.

"I tried!" she said, defensively. "I called him and there was no answer. I went over to his place, he wasn't there. I left a note on his door, telling him to call. I went across the street and talked to Jordan and their mom – they haven't seen him. I even went over to the high school and looked for his truck, but it wasn't there."

"Where could he be?"

"I don't know," she admitted, "but all the paperwork's done for you to get discharged and they're bringing a wheelchair up for you. You ready to get home?"

I nodded.

"I brought you this," she said, producing the rod from my gun cleaning kit. It was made of three separate metal rods that screwed together – one after another – to create one long, thin rod that could be inserted into the bore of a rifle. "I didn't think a knitting needle was going to be long enough."

"Give me that!" I exclaimed. "You're a genius!"

"Of course I am," she smiled, and I scratched until the wheelchair arrived.

Laci obliged me by driving by Tanner's house and the high school again before we went home, but his truck wasn't in either place.

We got home and I couldn't believe how hard it was for Laci to help me get into the house. We went in through the garage where there were only three steps, but it was still a nightmare. It was obvious that I wasn't going to be going up the stairs to get to our bedroom for a good, long while, so Laci turned the sleeper sofa in our living room into a queen-sized bed. I stood there on my crutches watching her put fresh sheets and a blanket on it.

"Thank you," I said when she'd finished.

"You're welcome," she said. "Here, let's get you settled."

That was another big struggle because the bed was a whole lot lower than the hospital bed.

"I'm never going to be able to get up out of here again," I said as she helped me swing my legs around.

"Yes, you will," she assured me. "We'll get the hang of it."

"I doubt it."

"Why don't you try to get some sleep?" she asked. "You look awful."

"Thanks."

"I mean you look *tired*. Did you get any sleep at all last night?"

"Not much."

148

"Look," she said. "I'm going over to my parents' house to get the kids. You see if you can get some sleep while I'm gone."

"Will you bring me my phone and my laptop?"

"You need to sleep!"

"I will after you get back," I promised her.

"You're worried that you won't hear the phone, aren't you?" she asked and I nodded.

She brought me my phone and plugged the charger into a nearby plug. Then she brought me my computer and plugged that in too.

"I'll be back in a few minutes," she said, kissing me before she left.

"Thanks," I said, opening my computer.

I checked my messages, but found none from Tanner. I emailed Scott and explained to him what was going on and that I expected to be able to keep working as soon as I got all my equipment from my upstairs office relocated into the living room. Then I tried Tanner one more time and left him another desperate message.

Laci's parents didn't live far away and she was back with the kids soon. They were glad to see me and Dorito was fascinated by my cast.

"Can I sign it?" he wanted to know.

"Sure."

"I'm gonna be the first one to sign it!" he said excitedly as Laci handed him a marker.

"You're gonna be the *only* one to sign it if you write that big!" I complained. His *D* was the size of my hand.

"People have to be able to see it!" he explained.

Lily seemed more interested in the fact that the couch had turned into a bed. She stood up and then bounced down hard, laughing.

"Ow!" I said, wincing in pain.

"Whoa, whoa, whoa," Laci said, scooping her up. "No jumping on the bed, okay? That hurts Daddy's leg."

Lily looked at me.

"Come on, let's go upstairs and play and let Daddy sleep, okay?" Laci suggested. Lily stuck her lip out and tears came into her eyes.

"No," I told Laci, "it's okay."

"Come here," I said to Lily, holding my hands out to her. Laci handed her to me. "It's okay. You wanna lay here with Daddy and watch TV?"

She nodded and snuggled up next to me while I found one of her favorite cartoons that we had recorded. I turned the volume down very low.

"Will you please try to sleep now?" Laci asked, picking up my phone. "I'll keep this with me and I promise I'll wake you up if Tanner calls."

"There's not much battery left on it," I worried. She checked it.

"It's almost halfway charged already," she said. "I'll take care of it."

"Okay," I agreed, suddenly aware of how hard it was to keep my eyes open. I pulled Lily closer to me and buried my face into her hair, and then I fell sound asleep.

When I woke up, the TV was off, Lily was gone, and it was dark. I could see a light in the stairwell coming from upstairs and hear the faint sounds of Dorito giggling.

"Laci?" I called. The hallway light came on and Laci came down the stairs.

"He *still* hasn't called?"

"He actually did call," Laci said.

"You promised me you'd wake me up!"

"Well," she said, "he told me not to. He told me that he didn't have anything to tell you yet, but that he had a plan and that he'd call you as soon as he had some news."

A plan. I was laying here all busted up and not able to do anything to help Amber because of Tanner's last "plan."

"I wish you'd woken me up," I said.

150

"I'm sorry," she said, "but he really acted like he was busy and needed to go and he said he didn't have anything to tell you."

"What are the kids doing?" I asked.

"They're making you a get-well-soon card on the computer," she smiled.

"Can you hand me my scratcher thingy?" I asked, pointing at the gun cleaning rod.

She smiled and handed it to me.

"Has anybody else called?" I asked.

"Charlotte called and your parens and Jessica stopped by, but you were pretty sound asleep."

"What did Charlotte want?"

"She wanted us to come over for dinner tonight."

"When are we supposed to be there?"

"We can't go over there for dinner!" Laci protested. "I ordered a pizza!"

"Why can't we go?"

"Well, first of all, it took us half an hour just to get you into the house and onto the couch," she reminded me. "I can't even imagine trying to get you up out of here and back down the steps and then out into the car again without a nurse to help us. Second of all, you aren't exactly 'dinner guest' material."

"What do you mean?"

"I mean, you haven't had a shower since the day before yesterday. I don't even want to think about how we're going to tackle that, but until we do, you aren't going over to anyone's house for dinner."

"So they're having dinner without me," I said.

"Yes," Laci said. "I suspect that they will continue eating and stuff even though you've broken your leg."

I was quiet for a minute, looking down at my stupid cast on my stupid leg. Then I looked back at Laci.

"We've got another problem, too," I said.

"What now?" she asked.

"I've gotta go to bathroom."

151

I won't even get into that whole process, but after I was *finally* up and had gone to the bathroom, I hobbled out onto the deck. I managed to lean over into the hot tub and get the upper third of my body fairly clean. Then we ate pizza.

Even though I'd slept most of the day, I was still pretty tired and I decided to go to bed when the kids did.

"Do you want me to sleep here with you, or do you think you'll sleep better alone?" Laci asked me.

"I'll sleep a lot better if you're here with me," I said, and she crawled in next to me. I snuggled up next to her and buried my face into her hair like I had done with Lily that morning. It worked just as well as it had earlier, and soon I was sound asleep again.

~ ~ ~

TANNER CALLED A little after midnight.

"What?" I asked, as wide awake as I'd ever been.

"You need to get down here to the hospital," Tanner said.

"What happened?"

"Amber's here."

"In the hospital?"

"She's . . . she's okay," he said, hesitantly, "but you need to get down here."

"What happened?"

"Just get down here," Tanner said. "And bring some clothes that'll fit her. Come to the emergency room."

"What happened?" Laci asked.

"I don't know," I said, "but Amber's in the emergency room and Tanner said I need to get down there."

"The emergency room?"

"He said she's all right. I don't know what happened."

"Who are you calling?" she asked.

"Jordan," I answered, and she got out of bed to change into jeans and a sweatshirt.

"Jordan," I said when he answered. "Wake up."

"I'm awake."

"Are you at home?"

"Yeah."

"Can you get over here and watch the kids?"

And help Laci get me out of bed?

"Sure," he said. "I'll be right there."

He not only helped me get out of bed, but he helped Laci get me into the car.

"Wow!" Laci said as she backed out of the garage. "That was a whole lot easier with him helping!"

"Yeah," I agreed. "I'm gonna call him over every time I need to go to the bathroom."

153

Someone at the emergency room entrance helped Laci get me out of the car. There was a wheelchair handy, so I plopped down into that and Laci wheeled me into the waiting room and up to the admittance desk.

"We're here to see Amber Patterson," Laci told the receptionist. Tanner must have heard her because he stuck his head out of a doorway down the hall.

"Down here," he said, motioning to us.

Laci wheeled me down the hall and into the room where Tanner was waiting for us and where Amber sat in a chair, wearing a hospital gown. She was busy wrapping a gauze bandage around the leg of a stuffed dog.

"Hey, Amber!" I said, so glad to see that she really was okay.

Her eyes opened wide when she saw me and she scrambled off her chair and ran over to me, climbing into my lap.

Ow, ow, ow! But I didn't say it out loud or let her see me wince.

"What happened to your doggie?" I asked her. She leaned toward my head and cupped her hand to my ear.

"He broke his leg, too," she whispered.

"Oh," I said, smiling. "Tanner told you I broke my leg, huh?" She nodded.

"Look where Dorito signed my cast," I said, showing her. "He hardly left any room for anyone else to sign it, did he?"

She giggled silently and shook her head.

"You wanna see if you can find some room to sign your name?" I asked her. She nodded.

"All right," I said. "Tanner and I are gonna go find a marker and you wait here with Dorito's mommy. We'll be right back, okay?"

She nodded and crawled out of my lap.

Tanner pushed me out of the room and back down toward the receptionist's desk. The receptionist was gone.

"What happened?" I asked in a low voice. "Why's she in the hospital?"

"They needed to do some tests and stuff," Tanner said, reaching over the counter of the desk and pulling a marker from a cup.

"Tests?"

"Look, David," Tanner said, "I don't know if–"

"Hey, Coach?" I heard a voice say. I turned and saw a young police officer approaching Tanner.

"Hey, Jaron," Tanner answered.

"I just need you to read this statement over and then sign it. That way we can go ahead and press charges. 'Course, like I said, I can't see this thing ever making it to court, but . . ."

"But you're going to let social services know what happened, right?"

"Oh, yeah. I've already contacted them. Her case worker's on the way."

Great.

"Did you tell her what happened?" Tanner asked.

"I told her briefly," the officer said, "but I'll fill her in on everything when she gets here and make sure she understands."

"Understands what?" I interrupted. *"What happened?"*

"This is David," Tanner told the officer, as if that explained everything.

"Oh," he said, knowingly, "the tree climber."

"WHAT HAPPENED?"

"Coach here's a hero," the officer said, clapping his hand down on Tanner's shoulder. "That's what happened."

"No, I'm not," Tanner said.

"You risked a lot for that little girl in there," the officer disagreed, jabbing his thumb down the hall toward Amber's room.

Tanner just shook his head.

"Officer Donoho?" I heard a voice call. He turned and I saw Amber's social worker, Erin Lamont, walking toward us.

Her pace faltered when she saw me. She glared at me for a moment, but then turned her eyes back to the policeman and made a point of ignoring me as she started talking to him.

Tanner wheeled my chair halfway back down the hall toward Amber's room.

"Wait!" I said. "I still have no idea what happened!"

Tanner stopped pushing and stepped up beside me.

"Look," he said quietly, squatting down next to me, "I don't think you really *want* to know what happened, and besides, we don't have a lot of time for me to explain everything to you right now."

"Is that the lady that you pissed off?" he asked, nodding back in Erin Lamont's direction.

"Yeah."

"Well then, listen to me," Tanner said. "Amber's not ever going back to that house – not *ever*. I can guarantee it. So, they're going to have to find another family for her. Now, it seems to me that this is your big chance to show that lady what great parents you and Laci would be to Amber. Don't you think?"

I was still so confused, but I nodded.

"Good," Tanner said, standing back up and starting to push me again. "Now get back in there and play nice."

We got back into Amber's room and found that a nurse had helped Laci change Amber into an old sweat suit of Dorito's that we'd brought along. Poor Laci was more confused than I was, but by the time Erin Lamont stepped into the room, Amber had written her name on my cast and was drawing a puppy.

"Is that puppy going to have a broken leg too?" I asked.

Amber nodded and giggled.

"Hi, Amber," the social worker said.

Amber looked up and froze.

"Do you remember me?"

Amber gave a slight nod.

"How are you doing?"

Amber didn't move.

"Kind of a rough night?"

156

She still didn't react.

Erin Lamont crossed the room toward Amber and stooped down beside her.

"We're going to find you a nice home where that won't happen to you again, okay?"

She waited for Amber to nod, but Amber still didn't move.

"May I have this?" she asked, taking the marker from Amber's hand and snapping the lid in place. She thrust it in my direction and dropped it in my lap when I didn't take it from her.

"Let's go, honey," she said, taking Amber's hand and standing back up.

"Wait!" I said. "Can she please be placed with us? Please?"

"No," Erin Lamont said, shaking her head. "That's out of the question."

"Why?" Laci asked.

"I don't think that would be in Amber's best interest."

"Why not?" Laci wanted to know.

"There are many factors that go into deciding where to place a child. I'm not going to stand here and discuss—"

"Please?" Laci interrupted. "Please let her come and stay with us. We've already gone through the certification process and we're almost approved. We love her. Please let us have her."

"I'm sorry, Mrs. Holland," the social worker told her. "There are too many reasons why this would not be a good placement."

"What reasons?"

"Forget it, Laci," I said. "It's not gonna happen."

"What reasons?" Laci insisted.

"Well," she said, "quite frankly I feel that your husband has an unhealthy obsession with this child."

"What?" Laci cried.

I felt Tanner's hand grip my shoulder.

"Officer Donoho tried to assure me that you had nothing to do with the events of this evening," she said, "yet here you are. I find that odd. Actually, I find it more than odd. I find it suspect, and I think that your interest in this child is abnormal."

"Abnormal?" I asked. "You think it's *abnormal* that someone cares about a child and wants to protect her and love her and care for her?"

"David–" Tanner said, squeezing my shoulder harder. I tried to shrug his hand off.

"David would be a great foster parent for Amber," Laci insisted. "He has nothing but her best interest at heart. Both of us do."

"I really do hope that's the case," the social worker said insincerely, "but if I placed Amber in your home when I had such serious doubts . . . well, I really wouldn't be doing my *job* now, would I?"

"Don't give me that crap about doing your job!" I shouted.

"David!" Laci gasped.

I ignored her.

I stared at Erin Lamont. "You can't admit that you never should have put her in that home in the first place, and now you're going to keep her from me just for spite!"

"David!" Tanner warned, gripping my shoulder.

"Forget it, Tanner," I said. "She's not a big enough person to do the right thing. She doesn't really care what's best for Amber, as long as she doesn't have to admit that she was wrong for ever putting her in that home in the first place. She's nothing but a petty, spiteful–"

"DAVID!" Laci gasped.

"Come here, Amber," I said, reaching for her. She held out her free hand, but Erin Lamont pulled her further away from me.

"I just want to say goodbye to her," I glared.

"You can say goodbye to her from here."

Tanner took his hand off of my shoulder and stepped toward the social worker. He stood, towering over her and reached down for Amber.

"Come here, Amber," he said. "David wants to say goodbye to you."

He lifted her easily, breaking the grip the social worker had on her hand. Then he set her down gently onto my lap and I wrapped my arms around her.

158

I whispered in her ear how much I loved her and how much I was going to miss her. I told her that I was going to pray for her every day for the rest of my life and that I would never, ever forget her.

"I love you so much," I whispered. "Don't ever forget that, okay?"

Amber put her mouth to my ear and cupped her hand to whisper, but no sound came out. She sat back, looking dismayed.

"You want to tell me that you love me too?" I asked, and she nodded, tears welling up in her eyes.

"Don't cry," I whispered. "I know you love me. You don't have to say it. I know."

She hugged me tight and then Laci and Tanner said goodbye to her and Laci handed her the stuffed dog with the bandage on its leg and then Erin Lamont took her hand again and started leading her from the room. Amber looked back over her shoulder at me one more time before she disappeared out the door.

~ ~ ~

EVER SINCE THE day we got married, Laci and I have always prayed together. Down on our knees, holding hands, praying out loud. It had been Laci's idea – especially the part about being down on our knees – and it was something that we did every night when we were together.

I'll admit that at first it had seemed awkward and embarrassing, but I'd gone along with it because Laci had wanted to, and back then I'd have done just about anything that Laci wanted.

Now, it was something that I looked forward to every night. It was something I wanted to do. Something that I needed to do.

But we hadn't prayed together in almost a week – not since before she'd flown to Houston. Not since the night that Tanner and I had broken into the Exceptional Children's Services and stolen confidential files from their office. Not since the night I had decided that I knew better than God.

I didn't really know if I could bring myself to let Laci know everything that I'd done. Besides that, there was no way I was going to be able to kneel down and pray with this stupid cast on my leg. But there was so much I needed to pray about. I'd lied . . . I'd been hateful . . . I'd broken the law.

I locked myself in the bathroom and tried to talk to God by myself. But I was ashamed . . . and (to be honest) disappointed in God. A very poor combination, indeed.

Needless to say, it didn't go too well.

"David?" Laci called, rapping lightly on the door after I'd been in there for a while. I didn't answer.

"David?" More loudly this time, banging on the door.

"I'll be out in a few minutes," I told her, the sound of my voice betraying me.

"What's wrong?"

"Nothing."

160

In a moment, I heard the little metal key that we hid on top of all the door jams being inserted into the lock.

"I'm coming in," she warned as the handle turned. She waited for a moment, giving me a chance to protest, but when I didn't, she pushed the door open.

As soon as I saw her, I felt the tears come into my eyes. She looked at me sympathetically.

"David," she said softly, reaching for me.

"I can't even pray," I told her, choking on the words.

She pushed herself up onto the counter. "Come here," she offered, opening her arms to me. I leaned against her, letting her support my weight. She kissed my forehead.

I buried my head against her shoulder and we stood there like that – with her holding me – for a long time. Finally she said softly, "There's nothing you can't tell me."

And so, I told her everything.

When I was finished, I said, "I know what I did was wrong, and I know I don't deserve Amber, but none of this is *her* fault."

"She's going to be okay. God won't let her go through something unless it's going to work for good."

"I don't want her to go through *anything!*"

"He loves her even more than you do," she reminded me.

"I'm going to miss her so much," I cried, my head still buried on her shoulder.

"I know," she soothed quietly, stroking my hair. "I know you are."

And then Laci prayed. Out loud.

First she prayed for Amber. She prayed that God would take care of her and put her in a good home and draw her close to Him and that she would always know His peace.

And then Laci prayed for me – because she knew I couldn't pray for myself.

161

~ ~ ~

THE NEXT MORNING, Tanner and Jordan came over.
Together, they found a beam in the ceiling and installed a giant eye
hook. Then they threaded a length of rope through it and tied it off, a
loop at one end.

Laci came out of the kitchen, licking frosting off of her finger.

"How does this help?" she wanted to know.

"I can do a lot of the work now when I need to get up," I
explained, grabbing the rope and pulling. Laci hardly had to help at
all before I was standing, supporting myself on my crutches.

"This'll improve your upper body strength," Tanner said, flexing
his biceps. "Before long, you'll look like me."

"That's an incentive," I muttered.

Dorito jumped onto the bed, grabbed the loop and swung away
like Tarzan.

"No, no, no," Laci said. "I don't think that's a good idea."

"It's not gonna break or anything," Jordan assured her.

"It's not a good idea," Laci replied through gritted teeth.

"Oh, yeah," Jordan suddenly agreed, shaking his head at Dorito.
"It's not a good idea."

"Awwww." Dorito looked crestfallen.

"Come on," Laci offered. "You wanna help Lily decorate
Christmas cookies?"

"*I* wanna help Lily decorate Christmas cookies!" Jordan said, and
the three of them headed into the kitchen.

After they'd left, I hobbled over to the window and stared out
into the front yard.

"Wanna get some fresh air?" I asked Tanner.

"Sure."

He basically lifted me down the stairs and then handed me my
crutches.

"You're very handy to have around," I observed.

"Yup," he agreed as we started down the drive.

162

"Thanks for getting Amber out of there," I said when we reached the sidewalk.

"I'm sorry they didn't let you have her."

"She's out of there now," I said. "That's the most important thing."

"I guess," he agreed.

"I wanna know what happened," I told him, stopping and looking at him.

He stopped for a brief moment, but then he shook his head.

"No, you don't," he said, and he kept on walking.

"Tanner!" I shouted at him. He stopped walking again and turned to face me. "I want to know. I want you to tell me what happened."

"If I tell you," he warned, "you're gonna wish you'd never found out."

"It can't be as bad as all the things I'm imagining," I assured him.

He stared at me for a long moment and then walked back to where I was. Then he told me. And after he was done telling me everything that had happened, I discovered that he'd been right and that I should have listened to him.

I wished I'd never found out.

~ ~ ~

AFTER THAT, LIFE went on. Like Tanner had predicted, my upper body strength increased, and very soon I was able to get myself out of bed. One afternoon I even managed to scoot – on my butt – backwards up the stairs and get into the shower. With a garbage bag taped tightly over my cast, I took the first shower I'd had since I'd fallen from the tree six days earlier. I needed to get clean . . . we were getting ready to go over to the White's for Christmas Eve dinner.

As far as I could tell, Charlotte didn't know anything about the fight I'd had with Jacob. I think she couldn't wait for the two of us to get together.

"Be nice!" Laci warned before we left the house.

"I'm not making any promises."

"At least be civil!" she insisted. "For Charlotte's sake."

"I'll be civil if he is."

"That's real mature," she muttered.

We arrived at the White's house and I managed to hop up the stairs with my arm around Laci's shoulder. Mrs. White opened the door.

"Lasagna?" I asked, inhaling deeply as we entered the living room.

"What else?" Mrs. White smiled.

Charlotte came to the door to hug me. Looking over her shoulder, I saw Jacob, hanging back, leaning against the door to the kitchen.

"So, you guys have already met, right?" Charlotte asked, looking from Jacob to me. We both nodded. "Great! Well, everybody come on in and sit down."

"Dinner's almost ready," Mrs. White said, looking at me. "Would it be easier if we just went ahead and sat down in the dining room?"

"Yeah," I said, nodding. "Thanks. Getting up and down's the hardest part."

164

"Is Jordan coming?" Laci asked.

"No," Charlotte said, shaking her head. "Chase got in a few hours ago and Jordan just decided to stay home."

"So, he's able to drive?" Jacob asked.

"For right now," Charlotte said. "But, I saw him today and he's really having some problems. I don't know how much longer he's gonna be able to be on his own."

"Has Jordan decided if he's going to get tested?"

"Not yet," Charlotte said.

"Do you want him to get tested?" Laci asked her.

"Depends on when you ask me," she said. "I waver back and forth . . ."

"That's understandable," I said. "I don't know what I'd do."

"Charlotte?" Mrs. White called. "Could you come and help me with the salad?"

"I'll help," Laci offered, standing up and heading into the kitchen.

"Charlotte tells me you're an engineer?" Jacob asked, looking at me politely. He acted as if we'd had tea a week earlier instead of a fight, and I wondered if someone had warned him to be civil too.

"Yes, I am," I said. If he was going to be civil, then I was going to being civil too. I could be *way* more civil than he could. "How about you, Jacob? What do you do?"

"Well, I'm on disability right now," he explained, "but before I got sick I worked for Schaffer Technologies."

"X-rays?"

"Right," he nodded.

"How'd you know that?" Charlotte asked.

"Because, a lot of times we use X-rays to determine the integrity of metal supports that are in concrete," I told her. Then I asked Jacob, "What was your position?"

"Medical division, maintenance and support."

I nodded.

I'll bet he has an associate's degree at best. Big deal.

"Isn't that neat?" Charlotte wanted to know.

"Uh-huh," I nodded as Laci set some salad dressing down in the middle of the table.

"I mean," she went on, "Dad was a physics teacher and I'm going into engineering and Greg was going into engineering . . ."

"It's a little bit different," I said to Charlotte, carefully. "I mean, engineers *design* stuff . . ."

"Yeah," Jacob agreed. "My job is just to fix and maintain things . . . even if they were engineered poorly."

All right, that's it.

"Look!" Mrs. White said, a little too cheerily. "The lasagna's here! Lasagna is David's favorite!" she told Jacob. "Ever since – what was it, David? Seventh grade?"

I nodded.

"Ever since seventh grade," she went on, "he's always loved my lasagna."

"Here," Laci said, setting a bowl of salad down on the table and thrusting a pair of tongs at me. "Dish up your salad."

I took the tongs from Laci and put some salad on my plate.

After we'd said grace, Jacob tried his hand at being civil again.

"So," he asked, "how exactly did you break your leg? Something about getting a Frisbee out of a tree?"

I glanced at Laci and then I shook my head. I wasn't going to lie anymore – not even to Jacob.

"No," I said. "Not exactly. I wasn't playing Frisbee."

"What happened then?" Charlotte asked, surprised.

"I'd really rather not talk about it right now," I answered.

Charlotte let it drop, but she narrowed her eyes at me and I knew she was going to pester me about it later. That was fine – I'd tell her and Mrs. White – but it was none of Jacob's business.

"So, Jacob," Laci said, "where did you grow up?"

I shot her a thankful look for changing the subject and she smiled at me.

"Mostly in the northeastern part of the state."

"What town?"

166

"Different ones," he shrugged and hesitated. Then, he finally said, "I kinda got bounced around a lot."

Charlotte looked at me and Laci.

"Jacob spent a lot of time in–" Then she stopped and looked at him, laying her hand on his arm. "You don't care if they know, do you?"

He glanced at Charlotte and then looked directly at me.

"My mom was pretty messed up," he said. "I got taken away from her a lot. She'd get her act together for a while and then I'd get to go back to her, but then she'd screw up again and the state would take me away again."

"I . . . I didn't know that," Laci said. "I'm sorry."

He shrugged again.

"Were you ever in foster care?" I asked.

"Yeah," he nodded. "I was in foster care a lot."

"So you got placed with different families?"

"Yeah."

"Was it . . . I mean, were they *good* families?"

"Yeah," he said. "I had real good families."

I looked at Laci and smiled. She smiled back.

Charlotte raised her eyebrows at us.

"What's that all about?" she asked us.

"We tried to take in a little girl who was in foster care, but we didn't get her," Laci answered.

"Why not?"

"Because," I said, "basically her caseworker hates my guts and she's pretty much made it her personal mission in life to make sure that I never see Amber again."

"That's not right!" Charlotte cried.

"No," I argued, "actually it is. I was really rude to her and I did a lot of things I shouldn't have done. I got what I deserved."

"But," Laci interjected, putting her hand on mine, "we're very hopeful that Amber's in a good home now, and it's really comforting to hear Jacob say that he was placed with good families."

"Well, to be honest," Jacob said, "I was more fortunate than most kids."

"What do you mean?" I asked.

"My caseworker was really good," he said. "She was in charge of me from the time I went into foster care when I was three until the time I aged out and she was great. She really went out of her way for me. You know, above and beyond the call of duty, that sort of stuff."

"What do you mean?"

"I dunno," he said. "She just really seemed to like me – I was her favorite kid for some reason – or at least she made me feel like I was. She always made sure I had good families and she checked on me all the time and everything. I've been out of the system for *fifteen* years and she still keeps in touch with me and wants to know how I'm doing and stuff. Most foster kids aren't that lucky."

Charlotte looked at him and nodded subtly in my direction.

"But," he added quickly, "I'm sure this girl . . . what's her name?"

"Amber."

"Right," he nodded, "Amber. I'm sure Amber's in a great home."

"I didn't know about any of this," Mrs. White said.

"I know," I said. "I just haven't really wanted to get into it."

"I'm sorry."

"It's okay," I said. "But I'd rather talk about something else."

"Sure."

"When are you going to get tested, Charlotte?" Laci asked.

"I got tested on Monday."

"Already?"

"Yeah."

"What'd you find out?"

"We won't get the results back for a week or two," she said.

"What happens if you're a match?" Laci asked.

"Then Jacob will check into the transplant center here in Cavendish and he'll go through this . . . what's it called?" she asked him.

168

"Preparative regimen," he said.

"Right. Chemo and radiation. It'll get rid of all the cancerous cells. Then he'll get my good cells and *voilà!*" She snapped her fingers. "We all live happily ever after."

"What if Charlotte's not a match?" Laci asked Jacob.

"Then I'm probably going to have to go to Iowa City or Chicago. The transplant center here in Cavendish doesn't do transplants from non-related donors."

"I'm going to be a match," Charlotte said, smiling at Jacob. "I can tell."

~ ~ ~

TEN DAYS LATER – the day before Jordan was set to fly back to Texas and the day before Charlotte was supposed to drive back to State – Charlotte's bone marrow results came back.

"Five out of six markers!" she said excitedly when she called to tell me.

"So what's that mean?"

"It means he can use my marrow!"

"But weren't there people on the registry who were five out of six?"

"Yeah," she said. "What about it?"

"Well, you need to just let one of those people donate. You don't need to be going through this right now."

"Going through what?"

"Look," I said. "Donating marrow can be very dangerous. You have to go under anesthesia and that's always dangerous, and I read about this man who donated and he got an infection in his blood and he died from it and . . ."

"David," Charlotte laughed. "They hardly ever harvest it that way anymore. All they're gonna do is take some blood. It's just like donating platelets."

"You should let somebody else do it. You've got school to think about."

"It's not going to interfere with school," she insisted. "But even if it did, school can wait! This is a once-in-a-lifetime chance to help somebody. And not just *somebody* – it's my brother. Plus, this way he can stay right here in Cavendish. I don't want him going all the way to Iowa City or Chicago!"

"He's your *half*-brother, Charlotte. You happen to share a little DNA with him – that's it. You barely even *know* this guy."

"I know him! I've spent the last two weeks getting to know him!"

170

"You can't get to know somebody in two weeks," I argued. "You don't know anything about him! What if he's got a record?"

"A record?"

"Yeah. Have you checked to see if he has a record?"

"No I haven't checked to see if he has a record!"

"Well, you should," I said. "He could be a criminal."

"He's not a criminal!"

"He could be . . . mentally unbalanced."

"What?"

"He said himself that his mom was really messed up. I'll bet she did drugs when she was pregnant with him. Plus, he spent his childhood in and out of foster care! You think he came out of all that unscathed?"

"What are you talking about?" she cried.

"He could have some real psychiatric problems. Who knows what's going on in his head? He could be schizophrenic or psychotic or–"

"What?"

"I'm saying you don't know anything about him. For all you know, he could be completely crazy!"

"*You're* completely crazy!" Charlotte answered.

The next day, as soon as Laci left to take Dorito to school, I called Jacob.

"Hi," he said, clearly suspicious.

"Charlotte tells me she's a match."

"Yeah," he said.

"I'm worried about her," I said. "I don't think she should do it."

"She told me that."

"She did?"

"Yeah," he said. "She told me you were worried about the procedure, but I thought she told you that it isn't invasive?"

"She did," I said.

171

"Then what are you worried for?"

"Because I care about her," I said. "I don't want anything to happen to her."

"I don't want anything to happen to her, either," he said. "I care about her too."

"Really?"

"Of course, really!" he said defensively.

"If that's true," I said, "then you won't let her do it."

"Why not?"

"Have you thought about what's going to happen if you don't make it?" I asked him quietly.

"What?"

"I mean, I . . . I really, really hope this works and everything and that you wind up going into complete remission. I really do, but . . ."

"But what?"

"There's a chance this isn't going to work, right?"

"Yeah."

"How much of a chance?" I asked.

"About a twenty-five percent chance."

"A one-in-four chance that it *won't* work?"

"Yeah."

"And if it doesn't, how do you think Charlotte's gonna take it?"

He didn't answer.

"I've been reading up on this," I said. "You know that when it's an anonymous donor some transplant centers don't even let them know how the recipient does for a year?"

"Yeah," he said.

"You know why?" I asked.

"Yeah."

"Because," I said, deciding to tell him even if he thought he already knew, "when somebody donates their marrow and then the patient dies, the guilt they feel can be devastating to the donor."

"I know," he said quietly.

172

"So, have you thought about that?" I asked him. "Have you thought about what Charlotte's going to go through if she donates to you and then you don't make it?"

"No," he said, still very quietly. "I guess I hadn't thought about that."

"Why don't you get it done somewhere else?" I said. "Then, in a year or so – after you know you're gonna make it – you can come back and get to know her . . . after there's not so much chance that she's gonna get hurt, you know?"

He was quiet.

"I mean, if Charlotte was a perfect match," I went on, "if your chances were better with her being you're donor, I'd say 'Go for it.' You know?"

"Yeah."

"But, if it doesn't improve your chances any . . . it seems like Charlotte could really get hurt. You know?"

"Yeah," he said again. "I hadn't thought about it like that."

"I'm not trying to tell you what to do," I insisted. "I just think that we need to really be thinking about Charlotte."

"Yeah," he agreed. "Maybe you're right."

~ ~ ~

CHARLOTTE CALLED ME. She was *livid.*

"Did you try to convince Jacob that he should get his bone marrow transplant from someone else?" she cried.

What an idiot. He was supposed to just get out of town and get out of Charlotte's life . . . not *talk* to her about it first.

"Charlotte," I said. "I just don't want to see you get hurt. I know you want to do this, but I think it would be best if–"

"I don't remember asking you what you thought."

"Look, Charlotte," I said. "I'm worried about you, and I think you're too close to this situation to look at it objectively."

"What's that mean?"

"I know you're excited to have found Jacob, but you're not thinking clearly. You don't even know if you can trust him! You're not protecting yourself."

"From *what?*"

"From . . . from all sorts of things."

"Like what?"

"Like . . ." I blurted out the first thing that came to my mind. "Like, what about your trust fund?"

"What about it?"

"Well, if he finds out that you have a trust fund that was set up because your dad was killed, he might just decide that since it was *his* dad, too, that maybe half of it should belong to him."

"That's ridiculous."

"No, it's not," I said.

"For your information he already *knows* about my trust fund and he hasn't said one word about it wanting any of it!"

"*You told him about your trust fund?*" I covered my eyes with my hands and groaned. "You and your mom need to go talk to a lawyer."

"I don't need to talk to a lawyer!"

"How long do you think it's gonna be before he decides that half that money should be his?"

174

"Maybe it should be," she said defiantly. "My dad didn't know about him, but I bet if he had, he would've made sure that Jacob was taken care of. Actually, now that I think about it, I think that half of that money probably *does* belong to Jacob!"

"Don't you dare give any of that money to Jacob!" I said, appalled.

"You can't tell me what to do," she yelled. "You're not my father!"

"I never said–"

"If I want to give him my bone marrow, I'll give him my bone marrow! If I want to give him my money, I'll give him my money!"

"Charlotte, I–"

Click.

She had hung up on me.

Over the next two weeks, Charlotte refused to answer her phone whenever I called. I even tried her on Laci's phone once, but as soon as she heard my voice, she hung up on me again. During this time, Jacob had intensive chemotherapy at the transplant center.

Charlotte came home on the weekends and spent every spare moment she had with him. She also came home on a Thursday, donated her marrow, and hung around the next day while Jacob received it. I found all this out from Laci, Tanner, and Mrs. White (all people with whom Charlotte was still on speaking terms).

Saturday – the day after the procedure – Tanner came by to play cards.

"Racquetball is a lot more fun than this," he complained.

"You're just sore 'cause I can beat you at this."

"How much longer 'til you get your cast off?"

"Well," I said, "Three weeks, but who knows when I'm going to be able to play racquetball?"

"Are you gonna help out again in Dorito's class after you're outta that thing?"

"I don't know," I said, shrugging and sweeping up the cards. "Amber's not in there anymore."

"She's not?"

"No," I said, shuffling the deck. "I think Erin Lamont moved her to another district just to get her away from me."

"I'm sure she's okay," he said.

"Yeah," I said. "Can we talk about something else?"

"Sure," he said, watching me shuffle cards for a minute.

"I saw Charlotte this morning," he finally said.

"You did?"

"Yeah," he smiled. "She sends her love."

"Seriously," I said, holding the deck tight. "What'd she say?"

"She said to tell you that she got pneumonia from the anesthesia and she's been coughing up blood and that she had a severe allergic reaction to the drugs they gave her and now she's got a blood infection from the IV and that's she's probably going to die."

"Very funny."

"She also said that she's going to flunk out of college."

I rolled my eyes and sighed.

"So, she's doing okay?"

"Yup. She and her mom are camped out in the waiting room at the hospital. I don't think she's going to leave until they find out if it worked."

"It's could be four weeks before they know that!"

"Yeah," he laughed. "That's why she's gonna flunk out of college."

"It's not funny, Tanner! This is what I've been saying all along – she needs to be back at college, studying and concentrating on her schoolwork. Ever since Jacob came into her life, her priorities are all screwed up. She's been completely forgetting about the things that are really important in her life!"

"Like you?"

"What?"

"Isn't that why you're so jealous of Jacob? Because you're afraid she's going to forget about you?"

176

"JEALOUS?"

"Yes, jealous."

"Of Jacob? I'm not *jealous* of Jacob!"

Tanner laughed. "You're kidding, right?"

"No, I'm not kidding."

"I can't believe you don't know how jealous you are."

"I'm not jealous!" I insisted.

"Are you sure?" Tanner asked. "He's Charlotte's brother."

"*Half*-brother."

"Yes," Tanner agreed. "You're always very quick to point that out. But the reality of it is, he's her brother and you're not."

"They share a little bit of DNA," I said. "So what?"

"And now they share a little bone marrow, too."

"So what, Tanner? That doesn't mean anything."

"Are you serious?" Tanner asked. "It means everything! I mean, everybody knows that ever since Greg and Mr. White died, you've really stepped in and tried to be like a brother to Charlotte, but . . . now that she's got another brother – a *real* brother – what's she need you for?"

"That's stupid, Tanner! That's the stupidest thing I've ever heard!"

"Yeah, it's stupid," he agreed, "but I think that's what your problem is. I think you're worried that Charlotte's gonna forget all about you or that she's going to choose Jacob over you or something – just because she's related to him."

"Well," I said, "she pretty much *has* chosen him over me, hasn't she? So if I am jealous, maybe I have every right to be."

"No," Tanner said, shaking his head. "She hasn't chosen him over you. She's just mad at you because you've been acting like a jerk. It doesn't have anything to do with Jacob."

I sat for a moment, thinking about what he'd said.

"I don't like him," I finally said quietly.

"You haven't given him a fair chance," Tanner answered.

~ ~ ~

WHEN I HAD been worried about Amber, I'd taken things into my own hands and tried to control the situation myself, never once asking God for help or guidance, even going against what I knew to be His will.

Now, here I was – just a few weeks after losing Amber – doing essentially the same thing . . . chasing after what *I* wanted, not asking God what *He* wanted, trusting in my own abilities instead of asking God for help, doing things that I knew He didn't want me doing. It was no wonder I was losing Charlotte too.

This time, when I locked myself in the bathroom to pray, however, things went much better.

I don't want to keep screwing up. Please help me to seek Your will first and then help me to know Your will and then help me to do Your will.

When Laci knocked on the door and asked me if things were all right, I was able to honestly tell her that they were.

"I want to go to the hospital and see Jacob," I told her after I'd opened the door.

"Now?"

"Yeah," I said. "Do you think your mom could watch the kids?"

"I'll find out," Laci said, pulling out her phone and heading upstairs. I made my way into the living room and sat down. A few minutes later, she came downstairs with the kids in tow.

"She said that's fine," Laci told me. "I'm gonna take them over there. Are you ready to go now or do you want me to come back and pick you up?"

"I just need a few more minutes," I told her.

"Okay."

They'd only been gone for a minute when my phone rang. I'd been planning on praying some more before going to see Jacob, and I almost ignored it. Almost.

"Mr. Holland?"

"Yes?"

178

"This is Stacy Reed with the Department of Social Services, Children's Welfare Division."

"Yes?"

"We have a child we'd like to place in your home."

"Oh," I said, "I . . . I don't know if my wife and I are actually interested in taking in a foster child right now. I mean, I know we applied and everything, but–"

"I believe you know this child," she interrupted. "She's an eight-year-old little girl? Her name is Amber Patterson?"

I could hardly breathe.

"Is this a joke?" I asked.

"No, sir. I have her paperwork right here in front of me."

"Wait. Who did you say you are?"

"Stacy Reed," she said again. "I'm a caseworker with the Department of Social Services, Child Welfare Divi–."

"But you're not Amber's caseworker . . ."

"I am now," she said. "My supervisor assigned her to me this morning and gave me specific instructions to call you for placement."

"Why?" I asked. I'd gone from not being able to breathe to hyperventilating. "What happened? Is she okay?"

"She's fine. I met with her and her current family about an hour ago and she's fine."

"Why are you moving her, then? I thought you didn't move kids unless there was a good reason."

"Quite frankly, sir, I'm not sure. My supervisor assigned her to me today and told me to contact you about placement."

"I can't believe this," I said softly.

"Are you interested?"

"What?"

"Are you interested in taking Amber in?"

"Yes!" I practically shouted. "Of course we're interested. We absolutely want her."

"Would you like to speak with your wife and then get back to me?"

"No, I don't need to speak to my wife. We want her. We'll take her right now."

Stacy Reed laughed.

"How about in the morning?" she asked. "I'll bring her by at about eleven o'clock. Does that sound okay?"

"Yes," I said. "That sounds wonderful."

"Very well," she said. "I'll see you then."

"Are you sure this isn't a joke?" I asked again.

"No, sir," she said kindly. "This isn't a joke."

"Would you tell Amber that we'll have tacos for lunch?"

"Tacos?"

"Uh-huh."

"Sure," she said. "I'll tell her."

"Thank you."

"You're welcome, sir."

I hung up the phone and looked at the number again. I typed it into a reverse phone search on the computer and saw that the call had come from the Department of Social Services. Then I searched "Stacy Reed" and found several references to a caseworker with DSS.

I heard Laci coming in through the garage.

"LACI!" I hollered, getting myself out of the chair with one strong pull on the rope. "LACI!!"

"What?" she asked, running into the house. "What's wrong?"

"Nothing's wrong!" I said, supporting myself on a crutch with one arm and wrapping the other one around her. "You won't believe what just happened . . . you won't believe it!"

"What?"

"Amber's coming to live with us! Tomorrow morning!"

"WHAT?"

"Someone from DSS just called and they're going to place her with us and they're bringing her here *tomorrow!*"

"*What?* Why? What happened?"

"I don't have any idea," I admitted. "All I know is that we're getting her! She's coming here tomorrow and she's going to live with us!"

180

"I can't believe it. Are you sure about this, David?" Laci asked. "Maybe there's a mix-up or something."

"No," I said. "I'm sure, I'm sure! I don't know how it happened, but it did."

"God," she told me, smiling. "That's how it happened."

I smiled back at her and she hugged me.

"You ready to go to the center?" she asked.

"Oorah!" I said. "Let's go."

When we arrived at the transplant center, we found Mrs. White alone in the waiting room.

"Where's Charlotte?" I asked.

"I made her go home and take a shower," she explained. "She wants to spend every waking minute here."

"How's he doing?" Laci asked.

"He's . . . I think he's feeling pretty uncomfortable from all the chemo, but he's not complaining or anything."

"Do you think it would be okay if I went in and saw him for a little bit?"

"I'm sure that'll be fine," Mrs. White said. "Let me go check with the nurse."

In a few minutes, I had scrubbed and was wearing a facemask and a sterile paper suit that fit surprisingly well over my cast.

"You have a visitor," the nurse told Jacob after I'd hobbled down the hall behind her.

He was lying on his hospital bed behind a plastic barrier.

"Oh, hey!" he said when he recognized me.

"How are you feeling?"

"Pretty good," he said. "Nervous, I guess. It's gonna be a long three weeks until we find out."

"I'll be praying for you," I promised.

"Thanks," he nodded.

"Um, so listen—"

"You wanna sit down?" he offered, pointing to the chair that was next to me.

"No," I said, shaking my head. "I'd probably never be able to get back up again."

"Okay."

"I just . . . I just wanted to apologize for the way I've been treating you."

"We didn't get off to the greatest start," he conceded.

"No," I agreed, "but even after that I . . . I've been a real jerk and I'm sorry. I'm really, really sorry."

"It's okay," he said. "I was too. Don't worry about it."

"Charlotte's one of the most important people in my life," I told him.

"I know."

"And, I guess when I found out you were her brother . . . well, I guess I was jealous."

"Jealous?"

"Yeah."

"You were jealous of me?"

"Yeah."

"*Why?*"

"I don't know," I shrugged. "I guess I was worried that she wouldn't need me anymore . . . that you'd take my place."

"Are you kidding?" he laughed. "She talks about you all the time!"

"She does?"

"You're like a superhero to her or something. She's always going, 'David this' or 'David that'! All I ever hear about is how great you are."

"Really?"

"Yeah," he laughed. "If anybody around here needs to be jealous, it's me, not you."

"She's not too thrilled with me right now," I smiled.

"No," he agreed, "I don't know what you did, but you're pretty much in the doghouse right now."

182

"She didn't tell you why?"

"No."

"Good," I said. "It was really stupid."

"I'm sure she'll get over it. I haven't known her all that long, but it seems to me like when she gets upset, she's the kind of person that just needs to take it out on someone and then she eventually gets over it."

"You've got her pegged pretty good."

I smiled at him through my mask and he smiled back.

"Well," I said, "I guess I'm gonna let you rest and see if I can go grovel my way back into her good graces."

"Good luck with that," he said, raising an eyebrow skeptically.

"Thanks," I said. "But listen, I want you to know that I really am sorry."

If there hadn't been a plastic, sterilized barrier between us, I would have offered to shake his hand.

"No problem," he nodded, giving me a thumbs-up sign and a smile. "We're good."

"If you're going to act like Greg's brother," I said, "you're gonna have to come up with some better hand signals than that."

"Huh?"

"I'll fill you in later," I smiled. "After you're all better, you and Charlotte can come over and have tacos and I'll tell you all about it."

"Okay," he said, acting mildly confused. "Good night."

"Good night," I said, and I hobbled out of the room.

Charlotte was in the waiting room when I got back, sitting next to her mother and Laci. Her hair was wet and she was glaring at me.

"Did you club him in the head with one of your crutches?" she wanted to know.

"No," I said, taking off my mask. "I smothered him with a pillow. There's a lot less mess that way."

Mrs. White suppressed a smile.

"Laci, why don't we go and get some coffee and leave the *children* alone for a few minutes?" she asked.

"Okay," Laci nodded.

"Try not to make the nurse call security," Mrs. White told us.

Charlotte watched them leave and then she turned and narrowed her eyes at me.

"What are you doing here, David?"

"I came to see Jacob," I said, tearing off my paper suit.

"Well, now you've seen him. Why don't you go home?"

"We need to talk first," I told her.

"I don't want to talk to you right now," she said, crossing her arms. "I want to go and see how Jacob's doing."

"He's fine. I just saw him. He's fine."

"Well, if you don't mind, I think I'll just go and see for myself."

She started to leave.

"Charlotte, wait!"

"What?" she asked, wheeling back around to face me.

"I came here to apologize."

"If you want to apologize to someone, you should apologize to Jacob!" she said, waving her arm in the direction of his room.

"I did."

"You did?"

"Yes."

"Really?" she asked, taking a step toward me.

"Yes, really," I nodded. "And now I want to apologize to you."

She looked at me for a long moment.

"Do you want to sit down?" she asked, gesturing toward a couch.

"I don't know . . ."

"I'll help you," she offered, stepping even closer.

"Okay," I agreed.

She helped me sit down on a couch and then she sat next to me.

"So," I said, "I told Jacob why I've been acting like such a jerk."

"Tell *me* why," she said quietly, tears forming in her eyes.

"Charlotte," I said, taking one of her hands and looking at her for a moment, "I've known you ever since you were this tall." I held my other hand a few feet off the ground. "I've watched you grow up, you're Greg's sister, you . . ."

184

I shrugged.

"You're one of the most important people in my life," I finally said.

"You're one of the most important people in my life, too."

"I know," I said, "but somehow I guess I just thought that if Jacob was around that . . . that you wouldn't need me anymore."

"What?"

"I was jealous," I shrugged again. "He's your brother. I'm not. It bothered me."

She looked at me for a long moment and then wrapped her arms tightly around me and buried her head against my shoulder. I hugged her back.

"You're so stupid," she finally said, wiping a tear away as she sat back.

"I know," I sighed, tapping my cast. "I've been doing a lot of stupid things lately."

"When are you gonna tell me the real story behind that?" she asked.

"Not tonight," I said. "But guess what?"

"You're getting Amber!"

"Oh," I said. "Laci told you."

"No," she replied. "Jacob did."

"Jacob? What are you talking about? How would Jacob know?"

"Jacob's the whole reason you're getting Amber, silly! Didn't he tell you that?"

"Tell me what?"

"That he called Ms. Maggie – you know, his old caseworker? He told her all about you and Laci and how much you wanted Amber and everything and she got it all worked out."

"What? Some caseworker that lives four hours away got Amber for me?"

"She's not a caseworker anymore, you dodo head. She's a regional director."

"A regional director?"

"Yeah, she's like over a third of the state or something now. So, anyway, Ms. Maggie talks to the regional director for our part of the state and *voilà!*" Charlotte grinned and snapped her fingers like she'd done on Christmas Eve. "Now you're getting Amber!"

I looked at her in disbelief.

"I . . . I can't believe Jacob's the reason I'm getting Amber," I finally said. "I've gotta go back in there and thank him."

I started to struggle to get up.

"Wait, wait, wait!" Charlotte said, grabbing my hand. "I've got some good news of my own!"

"You do?"

"Yeah." She held up her left hand and waved a sparkling diamond ring at me.

"Oh, wow! *Wow!*" I said, giving her a huge hug. "Congratulations!"

"Thanks!"

"When are you getting married?"

"Soon."

"You're not going to wait until you're through with college?"

"No," she said, tears welling up in her eyes again. "Life is so . . . so short and so unpredictable. We really couldn't think of a good reason to wait."

"What are you going to do about college?"

"He's going to transfer to State and we're going to get an apartment off-campus."

"What about his scholarship?"

"If he has a good spring in Texas, they might offer him one here. If not, well, then I just figured out what to do with some of my trust fund money."

"So, he's going to finish out the semester down there?"

"Yeah," she nodded, "and we're going to get married the last weekend in May."

She rapped her knuckle on my cast.

"Are you gonna be outta this stupid thing by then?" she asked.

"I'd better be! It's supposed to be off next month."

186

"Good," she smiled, "Because if you're going to give me away, I don't want you clunking along beside me while we walk down the aisle."

"Me? You want *me* to give you away?"

"Of course, *you!*"

"Really?"

"David, you're such an idiot sometimes," she said, shaking her head and smiling. Then she took my hand and looked at me, her eyes shining and bright.

"Honestly," she said, squeezing my hand. "Who else did you think I was possibly going to ask?"

Can just one family make a difference? Can just one person change lives for all eternity? Be sure to read the rest of the books in the *Chop, Chop* series to discover the full impact of Greg and his family in the years that follow.

Book One: *Chop, Chop*
Book Two: *Day-Day*
Book Three: *Pon-Pon*
Book Four: *The Other Brother*
Book Five: *The Other Mothers*
Book Six: *Gone*
Book Seven: *Not Quickly Broken*
Book Eight: *Alone*

On Facebook? Please be sure to become a fan of the *Chop, Chop* page to keep up with the latest!

For more information and free downloadable lesson plans, be sure to visit: www.LNCronk.com

Ordering five or more copies of any of the *Chop, Chop* books? Save 50% off the retail price **and receive free shipping!**

For details, please visit www.LNCronk.com or send an email to: info@LNCronk.com.

17168343R00118

Made in the USA
San Bernardino, CA
03 December 2014